# "Need any help dismounting?"

"I'm Texas born and bred, so no," she replied. But when her feet hit the ground, she found that her legs were a lot less sturdy than she'd thought. The honest truth was they were downright wobbly and she almost sank straight to the ground.

And she would have if he hadn't caught both her arms in an attempt to steady her.

"Careful," Jonah cautioned.

Embarrassed, Maggie murmured a stricken "Sorry about that."

"Nothing to be sorry about. You spent a day up a tree. You're lucky you still remember how to walk," Jonah told her.

There was a part of him that couldn't believe he was actually holding Maggie Reeves like this, the way he had once dreamed of doing. Usually, he found, dreams had a way of not measuring up to long-cherished expectations. However, in this case, holding Maggie Reeves against him was everything he had thought it would be—and more.

Her heart was doing a glorious, uninhibited dance in her chest and just for one wild moment, Maggie thought that Jonah was going to kiss her...

\* \* \*

Dear Reader,

Bellamy Reeves's and Donovan Colton's families were all gathering together in Whisperwood, Texas, preparing to celebrate the happy couple's wedding, when an unwanted guest crashed the anticipated ceremony. Hurricane Brooke came barreling through the small town and its surrounding area, destroying buildings in its path and unearthing secrets that had long been hidden. Specifically, the body of Emmeline, the town police chief's baby sister. Emmeline had been missing for close to forty years and was thought to be the victim of the town's infamous serial killer, who, coincidentally, was Maggie Reeves's former uncle-in-law, now imprisoned and serving several life sentences for murdering six young women.

On the day before the wedding, Maggie received a mysterious note sent to her by her late father-in-law. After following the map that had been sent with the note, Maggie literally found herself stranded up a tree when the hurricane hit. Jonah Colton, part of the Cowboy Heroes search-and-rescue team and there for his brother's wedding, rode out to find her. He hadn't expected to find the woman of his dreams as well, but nature had a funny way of bringing them together. Not that Jonah was complaining. Along the way to professing their love for one another, the duo survive a prison riot and Maggie's ex-husband, who is determined to make Maggie pay for leaving him. Have I gotten your attention yet?

As always, I thank you for taking the time to pick up one of my books, and from the bottom of my heart, I wish you someone to love who loves you back.

All the best,

*Marie Ferrarella*

# COLTON 911: COWBOY'S RESCUE

Marie Ferrarella

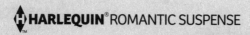
HARLEQUIN® ROMANTIC SUSPENSE

Special thanks and acknowledgment are given to Marie Ferrarella for her contribution to the Colton Search and Rescue miniseries.

ISBN-13: 978-1-335-66206-4

Colton 911: Cowboy's Rescue

Copyright © 2019 by Harlequin Books S.A.

PLEASE RECYCLE — THIS PRODUCT IS RECYCLABLE

Recycling programs for this product may not exist in your area.

Printed in U.S.A.

HARLEQUIN®
www.Harlequin.com

*USA TODAY* bestselling and RITA® Award–winning author **Marie Ferrarella** has written more than two hundred and fifty books for Harlequin, some under the name Marie Nicole. Her romances are beloved by fans worldwide. Visit her website, marieferrarella.com.

### Books by Marie Ferrarella

### Harlequin Romantic Suspense

### *Colton Search and Rescue*

*Colton 911: Cowboy's Rescue*

### *Cavanaugh Justice*

*Mission: Cavanaugh Baby*
*Cavanaugh on Duty*
*A Widow's Guilty Secret*
*Cavanaugh's Surrender*
*Cavanaugh Rules*
*Cavanaugh's Bodyguard*
*Cavanaugh Fortune*
*How to Seduce a Cavanaugh*
*Cavanaugh or Death*
*Cavanaugh Cold Case*
*Cavanaugh in the Rough*
*Cavanaugh on Call*
*Cavanaugh Encounter*
*Cavanaugh Vanguard*
*Cavanaugh Cowboy*

Visit the Author Profile page at Harlequin.com for more titles.

To
Patience Bloom
For Always Being
My Guardian Angel

# Prologue

*The truth shall set Elliott free.*

Maggie Reeves, formerly Maggie Corgan, had always been cursed with an insatiable curiosity. The slightest hint of a mystery could set her off. Which was why she was out here, in the middle of Live Oak Ranch—a ranch that belonged to her ex-husband's family, a local ranching dynasty—following a map that she had propped up beside her on the passenger seat, when she should have been back in town, getting ready for her sister's wedding.

Granted, the wedding was tomorrow and logically, there was plenty of time for her to get ready, even if she moved in slow motion. That was the argument Maggie had used on herself to assuage her conscience when she couldn't seem to tamp down her curiosity.

The wind was picking up. She pushed her blond hair out of her eyes and focused again on the road ahead. So many questions filled her head, it was hard keeping them straight.

Why would her ex-husband's late father leave her anything in his will? Yet according to her attorney, Adam Corgan had addressed the envelope to her, saying it was to be sent to her upon his death. When Maggie opened it, she had no idea what to expect, but it certainly wasn't a map of his property highlighting "the tallest live oak" with an X.

There was a note included with the map. She had read and reread the note a dozen times. As written, it was simplicity itself.

She just didn't understand it.

*The truth shall set Elliott free.*

What was that supposed to *mean*? What truth?

She knew who Elliott was. *Everyone* knew who Elliott was. Elliott Corgan was Adam's disgraced older brother. He had suddenly disappeared years ago, his location a secret that his family guarded closely. No one within the family spoke about him, but over the years, there had been rumors.

It was the stuff that local legends were made of, some of it possibly true, some of it obviously not. It all depended on what a person believed and who was telling the story at the time.

After her divorce, Maggie didn't give Elliott Corgan any thought at all.

Until the letter had arrived.

But just what was this "truth" and how would finding it—whatever "it" was—set Elliott free?

Free in the biblical sense or actually free? And free from what? Why would the man she had never met need to be set free? She didn't understand any of it.

An even-bigger mystery, in her opinion, was why had her ex-father-in-law sent this to her after his death? They hadn't been particularly close when she was married to James. They certainly were less than that once she had divorced his son.

And yet, Adam Corgan had left specific instructions that this be sent to her after he died.

*Why?*

"One mystery at a time, Mags," she murmured, glancing over toward the map again.

According to the directions, the tree that Adam wanted her to closely examine was located smack in the middle of some pretty rough terrain. Her vehicle was not equipped with four-wheel drive. There were times she felt it barely had front-wheel drive. The only way she was going to be able to reach the tree was to walk the rest of the way across the field.

Maggie sighed. She supposed that was why she had worn boots, in case this sort of thing came up. If she had any real sense in her head, she would just turn around and go back. But unfortunately, her curiosity trumped sense each and every time.

She got out of the car. The wind was really picking up, she caught herself thinking as she leaned into the passenger side and pulled out the map. Folding it so that it was more compact and manageable, Maggie began to make her way toward the tree.

She assumed that "setting Everett free" was probably going to require some digging. Well, she could do that when she returned after the wedding. For now, all she wanted to do was find the right spot.

Once she satisfied her curiosity—or at least as much of it as she was able to satisfy—she'd come back later on in the week. At that point she would do whatever needed to be done in order to discover this so-called "truth" that Adam Corgan had entrusted her with finding from beyond the grave.

"All very creepy if you ask me," Maggie stated out loud, even though there wasn't a soul around for what seemed like miles.

"Speaking of creepy," Maggie murmured, reacting to the wind, which was making a really mournful, increasingly loud noise now.

Feeling uneasy, she looked around several times to assure herself that it *was* the wind and not someone, or worse, some*thing* that was howling like that. It almost sounded like a wounded animal.

But it wasn't.

Finding out that it *was* the wind that was making such a racket and blowing so hard didn't really comfort her as much as it should have.

By the time she came close to her destination, Maggie realized that the world around her, which had been fairly bright earlier, had suddenly turned dark and foreboding, as if a giant switch had been flipped.

Maggie stopped trudging over the rocky terrain

about a foot shy of the tree her ex-father-in-law had marked and looked up at the sky.

The Texas sun had totally disappeared and the sky was beyond gray, almost black. The wind continued to pick up and was now making a really fierce noise.

That was when she suddenly remembered hearing something about a hurricane prediction. She had initially discounted it because half the time the weather bureau was completely wrong in its forecasts. Another 25 percent of the time, it was still off its mark by more than half.

"Why, of all possible times, did they have to pick *this* time to be right?" Maggie cried out in total exasperation.

The hurricane was no longer just a prediction. It was here. And getting worse.

Maggie quickly scanned the area. There was absolutely no place for her to hide. No place for her to take shelter from the coming storm.

And the hurricane, Maggie realized as she looked to her left, was coming straight at her.

# *Chapter 1*

When it was raging at its worst, Hurricane Brooke was gauged at having winds that were blowing through Whisperwood and its surrounding area at over 125 miles an hour, making it almost a category four hurricane. Taking the Texas town totally by surprise, the death toll quickly mounted and was currently up to thirty-eight and rising with dozens more still missing and unaccounted for.

A lot of Whisperwood's residents sought refuge in their basements, but others weren't so lucky. They were out in the open when the storm struck and scrambled for shelter anywhere they could, praying that shelter would hold.

Jonah Colton and three of his brothers had returned to the town where they were born a few days before the hurricane struck. At the time, they were all looking forward to seeing their brother Donovan become the first of their family to get married. As it turned out, three of the brothers belonged to Cowboy Heroes, a search and rescue team that scoured the countryside on horseback, rescuing people. They never dreamed they would have to put their skills to use in their own hometown, but things didn't always go according to plan.

And this was one of those times.

The moment the winds died down, before the hurricane was even officially declared to be over, Jonah, Dallas, Nolan and Forrest, a former police detective forced into retirement after sustaining a leg injury, were out, putting their acquired skills to good use, searching for and rescuing survivors.

Some of the houses in the area lucked out and were barely touched, but they quickly saw that others had been completely demolished. In some cases, the people who had lived in those houses were now buried beneath them in the rubble. Those were the people that Jonah and his brothers focused on helping first, bringing them to the church's recreational center, where survivors were being temporarily housed.

"You do a head count?" Jonah asked Forrest.

The latter, eight years Jonah's junior, had recently been forced to resign from the Austin Police Department when a bullet to his leg had left him incapacitated. Thanks to adhering to a diligent regiment of physical therapy, Forrest was now able to get around again, although he did have a pronounced limp. Unable to just do nothing, he had joined the volunteer search and rescue teams in order to feel useful. When the hurricane struck, he immediately volunteered to help find victims of the storm.

Jonah knew better than to insult his younger brother by treating him any differently than he would the other members of the team.

They had been at this now for over twelve hours without a break. Most of the people they had helped dig out had just sustained injuries, some more serious than others. But some of those they dug out would not be recovering. Those bodies were wrapped up as carefully as possible and placed out of sight until they could be taken to the morgue. Ironically, the morgue had been untouched by the hurricane.

Inside the rec center when Jonah had asked him the question about a head count, Forrest knew that his brother was referring to the members of their family. He was relieved to answer in the affirmative.

"Dallas found Mom and Dad. They're okay," he said, realizing that was the first thing that any of them would have asked. "So are Donovan and Bellamy," he told Jonah. "Nolan's supposed to be bringing them here," he added, looking around the rec center.

The recreation center was quickly filling up with people and cots at this point, but it was the largest common area available in Whisperwood. This was where town meetings were held, although the meetings had never drawn half this many people.

"There's no way we are going to be able to put up even *half* the town in here. There's got to be at least

5,500 people living in and around Whisperwood," Dallas Colton guessed as he walked into the center.

"We're sending the overflow to Kain's Garage and the General Store. They've got large storm cellars," Jonah told the others. "Hopefully, the storm's not going to be doubling back. Otherwise," he speculated as he looked from one brother to another, "the damage is going to be even worse than it is now."

"This really isn't so bad," Dallas commented, reviewing what he had seen in the last twelve hours. "Compared to other hurricanes."

Forrest frowned. "Try telling that to the families of the people who lost their lives in this," he said grimly.

Rehashing the situation served no purpose now. "You're right," Jonah agreed. "Help now, talk later," he told his brothers.

At that moment, Jonah spotted Donovan heading toward them, his hand firmly holding on to his fiancée's. Donovan appeared exhausted and he looked as if he could definitely use a change of clothes. His were wet and streaked with mud. Beside him, Bellamy appeared almost numb.

"Are you two all right?" Jonah asked, concerned that the woman next to his brother looked as if she was about to have a complete breakdown.

"I am, but—" Donovan began, but he never got a chance to finish.

Because at that moment, Bellamy grabbed Jonah's arm, clutching it as if she was holding on to a lifeline. The zombie look on her face vanished, replaced by an animated expression that looked as if it was actually bordering on hysteria.

"You've got to find her," Bellamy begged him with feeling.

"Her?" Jonah repeated, unsure of who the woman was referring to.

"Magnolia—Maggie—my sister," Bellamy almost shouted before she was able to get herself under control. "Please," she pleaded, still clutching his hand and squeezing it hard for emphasis. "She's out there somewhere, maybe hurt, or—"

Bellamy couldn't bring herself to utter the condemning word. It was just too frightening to give voice to. Instead, she repeated herself. "You have to find her and bring her back."

After years of being estranged, Bellamy and her younger sister, Maggie, had finally cleared up the misunderstanding, centered around their parents, that had kept them apart all this time. Bellamy had thought that Maggie had turned her back on the family to marry well and run off, when the exact opposite turned out to be true. When they finally sat down to talk, the truth came out. Issues had been resolved to the point that Bellamy had asked Maggie to be her co–maid of honor, along with her best friend Rae Lemmon. Maggie had happily agreed.

And now this happened.

"You *have* to bring her back," Bellamy insisted. "I can't lose her!"

"Where did you last see her?" Jonah asked, trying to retrace Maggie's steps.

Bellamy closed her eyes, trying to clear her head and summon the memory. It didn't come at first.

"At the house." Her eyes flew open. "The last time I saw her was at the house," she exclaimed.

"But she's not there." Donovan spoke up. "We went there are soon as we could," he explained to his brothers.

"Something awful's happened to her, I just know it," Bellamy declared, struggling to keep her tears back. "You have to—"

Still clutching his arm tightly, Bellamy was beginning to make his hand seriously numb. Even so, Jonah smiled reassuringly at his future sister-in-law.

"We will. We'll find her, Bellamy. I promise," he added. "But if I'm going to do that, I'm going to need the use of my arm," he told her, looking pointedly down at her hand.

Bellamy followed his gaze, totally oblivious to the fact that she was holding on to him so tightly.

"Oh," she cried, as surprised as he was that she was gripping his arm so hard. Belatedly, like a person waking up from a dream, she released her hold on him. Collecting herself, she asked, "You'll let me know the second you've found her? One way or the other, you'll let me know," she begged.

"If they get the phone lines working, I promise I'll let you know as soon as I find her," Jonah told Donovan's fiancée.

"As soon as *we* find her," Dallas corrected. "We're in this together, remember?" he reminded Jonah. "Don't worry," he told Bellamy. "Four sets of eyes are better than one." And then he turned toward Jonah again because there was no denying that Jonah was the team leader. "Just in case your superhero radar is off," he said, attempting to add just a little levity to what was a very dire situation.

"Spread out, guys," Jonah ordered, ignoring Dallas for the time being. "Before we go running off, beating the bushes for any sign of Maggie, let's find out if anyone here saw her or talked to her before this storm decided to redecorate the landscape. Plenty of people here to talk to," he added, gesturing around at the people who occupied the rec center. Still more were filing in by the hour.

Jonah felt he was getting nowhere. Questioning resident after shaken resident, he was forced to detach himself, putting up a wall between himself and those who were so very desperate to share their story with someone. He hated being so impersonal but needed to keep a clear head if he wanted to be able to find Maggie.

And he did.

Not just to keep his promise to Bellamy, but because he felt a special connection when it came to the woman he'd been tasked with finding. He remembered Maggie Reeves all too well from school, even though he was five years older than she was. He'd been a gawky kid back then, skinny as a rail until he'd started working on his parents' ranch in his teens. He'd filled out then, but Maggie, Maggie had been born beautiful and only grew more so as time went by. He remembered that she'd even won the coveted title of Miss Austin in a beauty pageant. There had been other accolades along the way. But that was before she had gotten married.

The marriage didn't last, but he could have predicted that if anyone had asked. James Corgan might have been wealthy, but he was an amoral alley cat. All the money in the world couldn't change that, Jonah thought as he continued questioning survivors. He never understood what Maggie had seen in James, but whatever it was, her vision cleared up soon enough and she had divorced him.

And now Maggie was out there somewhere, hopefully alive—

"Hey, Jonah, I found somebody who saw Maggie maybe an hour before the storm hit," Forrest called out.

Jonah looked up to see his brother trying hard not to limp as he made his way over. The former detective had Rae Lemmon with him. Adrenaline raced through Jonah as he instantly crossed to the duo, meeting them more than halfway.

"You know where she went?" Jonah asked the young woman with Forrest.

"I think so. Maggie talked to me just before she left." The petite brunette nodded, as if that added weight to what she was about to say. "She told me she was going to Live Oak Ranch."

Jonah looked at Rae, puzzled. "Doesn't that belong to her ex's family?" he asked the woman. Maybe Rae had gotten her facts confused. "Why would she be going there?"

Rae raised her slim shoulders in a helpless shrug. "I don't know. Maggie said she was going there because she needed to uncover a secret."

"A secret?" Jonah echoed, in the dark as much as ever. He glanced at Forrest, who just shook his head. He obviously didn't have a clue, either. "What secret?" Jonah asked the paralegal.

"I don't know," Rae repeated helplessly. "She wouldn't tell me anything. Maggie said she'd know more once she got there." And then Rae remembered something. "She did say she had a map."

"A map." Jonah was beginning to feel like a parrot, just repeating things that made no sense. He felt as if he'd been swallowed up by the hurricane and was now being tossed around without rhyme or reason. "Why would she need a map?" he asked. "Maggie lived on Live Oak Ranch when she was married to James, didn't she?"

"Yes," Rae answered. "But she took the map with her because she said she needed to pinpoint the biggest tree on the ranch." Rae shrugged again, feeling frustrated and helpless. She pressed her lips together, silently upbraiding herself that she hadn't made Maggie tell her more. "She really wasn't very clear, and I have to admit that I wasn't paying much attention to what she was saying. I was too busy going over last-minute details for the wedding," Rae confessed.

Rae flushed. The excuse sounded so weak now that she said it out loud.

"Not that it looks like that's going to happen now, at least not on schedule," she added in a small voice. Her tone shifted as she returned to the more important subject under discussion. She needed to tell Jonah anything that sounded even remotely relevant. The smallest thing could be instrumental in locating Maggie. "But I know Maggie—she gets something in her head, she doesn't let it go. I'm positive that she was there somewhere on the ranch when the storm hit."

"And you're sure about this?" Jonah pressed.

He was still somewhat skeptical about this information. After all, it had been a significant amount of time since Maggie had gotten divorced and she and her husband had gone their separate ways. From what he had heard, hers wasn't one of those divorces where the couple remained friends even after their marriage was dissolved. Maggie gave every indication that she didn't want to have anything to do with her ex.

So why would she suddenly go wandering around his family's ranch?

It didn't make any sense to him.

But sense or not, it was the only lead he had about Maggie's last whereabouts, so unless he found out something that was more immediate, he was going to act on this.

And he made up his mind that he was going to act on it alone.

"Absolutely sure," Rae told him solemnly. There was a slight hitch in her voice. "You're going to find her, right?"

"Right," Jonah replied without a moment's hesitation. "I'll find her." And he fully intended to do just that, even if it was the last thing he ever did.

More reports of missing residents were coming in even as Jonah stood there, listening to Rae. The volunteer search and rescue organization he and his brothers belonged to was already stretched to the limit, not to mention exhausted. He wasn't about to ask any of them for help, but he didn't plan on stopping until he located Maggie. The thought of her out there, stranded, possibly in danger and clinging to life, wasn't something he could live with if things took a turn for the worse.

Even if he hadn't already given his word to Bellamy and to Rae, he had made up his mind to do everything in his power to find Maggie.

By the sound of it, the wind was picking up again. Jonah looked out the rec center windows and saw the trees bending like flexible dancers before the oncoming winds.

Were they in for a second wave? It didn't matter, he thought. He knew he needed to get out there now, before traveling on horseback became hazardous and maybe even impossible.

"Thank you, Rae," he told the distraught woman. "You've been a great help."

She began to say something more, but he didn't have any time to waste. Jonah searched the area for someone he could charge with looking after Rae for now.

"Forrest," he called to his brother. The latter turned toward him after a moment, eyeing Jonah quizzically.

"Look after Rae, will you?" he requested. "She seems like she could use a friendly shoulder to lean on."

Forrest didn't look happy about the reassignment. "What about going to look for Maggie Reeves?" his brother asked.

"I got this," Jonah said, shrugging off the implied offer to help. "You take care of Ms. Lemmon and anyone else who might need you."

Forrest's face darkened as he took offense. "I was shot in the leg, Jonah, not the head. I'm perfectly capable of going out there with you to look for Bellamy's sister. Don't treat me like I'm an invalid," he warned his brother.

Jonah backtracked. "I know you're not an invalid," he said gruffly. He wasn't accustomed to trying to tread lightly around any of his brothers and doing so was tricky. "After you make sure Rae's taken care of, go out with the others and search for survivors. And I'll do the same," he declared authoritatively.

With that, Jonah headed out the door. He zipped up his rain slicker. Not that the outer garment would give him much protection if the storm got worse again. He supposed he was doing this more out of habit than anything else. If he followed a ritual, covering all the steps, maybe that would help him find Maggie.

*No stone unturned*, he thought.

Jonah hurried across the street toward what was left of the town's stable. He and his brothers had housed their horses here to keep them from being left out in the open once the storm hit.

Once inside, he made his way over to his horse,

a sleek palomino. Aside from the horses, there was no one around.

"How are you doing, Cody?" Jonah asked, taking time to interact with his mount before going out. He and Cody had been "partnered" for three years now. "Okay, boy, ready to play hero and earn your feed? I know, I know," he said as he put the saddle on his horse and tightened the cinches, "I don't want to go out, either. But there's a crazy woman out there who needs us because she doesn't have enough sense to come in out of the rain—or take shelter when a hurricane is predicted to come rolling through," he said, talking to the palomino as if he was a person. Taking the horse's reins in his hand, he swung into the saddle.

"Let's go do this. The sooner we find her, the sooner we can come back."

Cody whinnied as if he understood. Jonah never doubted that he did.

# Chapter 2

"I don't like this any better than you do," Jonah told Cody as he urged his horse on through the increasingly inclement weather.

He had been talking in a calm, steady voice ever since he and his horse had left the stable in Whisperwood. He wasn't sure if he was talking for Cody's benefit or his own, but it helped in both cases.

The farther away from Whisperwood he went, the more Jonah found that he had to steadily raise his voice, because not only had the wind picked up, but so had the threat of rain.

Actually, it wasn't a threat any longer. Rain had turned into a reality, falling with a vengeance. It would recede, only to return, coming down harder than it had before.

If this kept up, the chances of floods throughout the already-beaten-down area was a given. Jonah drew in his shoulders, trying vainly to stay dry. His rain slicker and Stetson were fighting a losing battle, but it wasn't in him just to give up. There was a woman out there who needed to be rescued.

"C'mon, where are you?" Jonah called out impatiently in his frustration.

He did his best to scan as much of the surrounding area as possible. According to his calculations, he had ridden onto the Corgan ranch about fifteen, eighteen minutes ago. Because of the rain that was still coming down, his visibility was limited. He hadn't been able to make out anything except for an occasional tree here and there. Certainly not a person.

In any event, Maggie wasn't near any of the trees he had made out.

"Maybe she's not here at all," he said to Cody. "And we're just wasting our time—not to mention that we're seriously running the risk of drowning out here if it gets any worse." Cody whinnied, as if agreeing with him. Despite the situation he found himself in, Jonah grinned. "I know, I know, we're the ones who don't have enough sense to come in out of the rain, not her. But legend has it Maggie's as stubborn as hell and if she said she was coming out here to find answers, this is where she probably is—but where?" he asked, frustrated.

Lowering his head, Jonah shoved his hat farther down on it, hoping to keep the wind from blowing it off.

"You see her, Cody?" he asked the palomino. "Because I sure as hell don't."

With one hand holding on to his hat, the other one wrapped around Cody's reins, Jonah raised up from his saddle, standing as best he could in his stirrups. He was blinking furiously to keep the rain out of his eyes as he scanned the area again, searching for a familiar shape, or some indication that Maggie was indeed out here, or at least had passed this way.

As he surveyed the area, Jonah realized that his horse had ridden in very close to this humongous oak tree. The tall, wide branches were offering him some degree of shelter from the rain—just in time, it seemed. The rain was coming down harder and harder now.

Some sort of natural reflex had Jonah glancing up over his head. It was not unheard-of for animals to go climbing up into the first available tree they could find. It was a self-preservation instinct to keep them from being swept away in a storm or a flood. The animals that he knew reacted this way were mountain lions—and bears.

The last thing he wanted was to be under a tree when a mountain lion or bear decided it wanted a snack more than it wanted to stay dry.

But when Jonah looked up, it wasn't a mountain lion or a bear that he saw.

*Maggie!*

*Thank God.*

"A little old to be climbing trees, aren't you?"

Jonah asked her, amused despite the less than ideal conditions they found themselves in.

Startled, Maggie had been so intent on holding on, she hadn't even realized that he was there.

"Oh lord," she cried, "you are the answer to a prayer!"

It had taken her more than a couple of moments to convince herself that she wasn't hallucinating. After all, she had lost track of how long she had spent up here in this tree. She could hardly believe that she was finally going to be rescued. And if that wasn't enough, this knight in shining armor was nothing short of gorgeous.

Part of Maggie wasn't fully convinced that she *wasn't* imagining all this. That she really *would* be rescued. Her arms had all but gone numb from hanging on to the branch she had climbed up on eons ago. At this point, she couldn't remember *not* being up here.

Jonah slowly angled Cody, as well as himself, right beneath the woman he had come to rescue. He wrapped the horse's reins around his saddle horn, then tightened his thighs about Cody's flanks so that he could hold his position as steadily as possible.

Having taken all the precautions he could, Jonah raised his arms. "Climb down," he instructed the woman perched above him. "Don't worry. If you slip, I'll catch you."

Maggie looked down uncertainly. She really had her doubts about his assurance. "That's a pretty tall order," she called back.

Jonah could appreciate why she was so uneasy. There were several feet of space separating her from his outstretched arms.

He reassessed the situation. "Are you going to make me climb up there and get you?"

It was more of a challenge than a question. Or maybe she was just interpreting it that way. Maggie didn't know. But she had never been the type of woman who would willingly cleave to the "damsel in distress" image. She wasn't the type to be rescued, either. She preferred doing the rescuing, the way she had tried to come through for her parents.

"Just hang on to your patience," she told him, slowly shifting her weight so that she could start to make her way down.

It took a second for her to release her grip on the branch, but she knew that it was either this or just staying where she was, clinging to a branch like some helpless female while this tall, dark and gorgeous specimen of a man played superhero. While that did intrigue her, it just wasn't her way.

Holding her breath, Maggie inched her way down.

The branch swayed and groaned with every move she made—or maybe that was the wind that was groaning. She didn't know. The only thing she *did* know was that she had to move slowly because there was no way in hell that she was going to come tumbling down out of this tree and wind up on the ground right in front of Mr. Magnificent's horse.

Watching her progress, Jonah grew steadily more uneasy. He continued to hold his arms up and opened.

The wind yanked at his Stetson, then ripped it right off his head.

"Damn," he muttered.

Maggie thought the remark was meant for her, but the next second she saw the cowboy's dark Stetson fly by her and then it disappeared into the darkened distance.

"I owe you a hat," she told her rescuer, raising her voice so that he could hear her above the howling of the wind.

"Just get down here," Jonah ordered, reaching up even higher. "We'll settle up later." His shoulders were beginning to ache. "You sure you don't want me climbing up there to get you?" he offered, watching Maggie's painfully slow descent.

"I'm sure!" she snapped, irritated that it was taking her so incredibly long to reach him.

It certainly hadn't felt as if it had taken her this long to climb *up* into the tree. But then, at the time, she'd been propelled by a dire sense of urgency. Maggie had been convinced that the floodwaters would just keep rising to the point that she would be in danger of being swept away.

Mercifully, they had receded and even though the rain kept falling, it didn't do so with anywhere near the intensity that the weather bureau had initially promised.

If it had, all of Texas would have been submerged by now, Maggie thought, inching her way down. And then she managed to reach the man who had come to her rescue.

"Sorry," Maggie apologized just as she finally reached Jonah's arms. "I really didn't mean to yell at you."

"Did you yell?" he asked, feigning ignorance. "I didn't notice."

Having succeeded in lowering her into the saddle, Jonah shifted so that he could position himself right behind Maggie.

Seated snugly, he closed his arms around her as he took hold of the reins again.

"Are you hurt?" he asked.

"Other than feeling stupid and having my pride wounded because I had to be rescued out of a tree? No," Maggie answered.

Taking a moment longer to remain under the tree and somewhat out of the direct path of the storm, Jonah considered her answer.

"Could have been worse," he told her.

Maggie found that she had to rouse herself in order to keep focused. Right now, she was losing herself in the warm feeling generated by having this hero's arms wrapped around her.

"How?" she asked, her voice sounding almost hoarse. She coughed, clearing her throat.

"You could have not known how to climb a tree," Jonah answered. He began to urge Cody to start heading away from the tree. The rain was just not letting up. "It looks like the floodwaters rushed through here before they receded back to a decent level."

"They did," she told him. "That's why I was up in the tree. I lost track of time," she ruefully admitted.

"Do you have any idea how long I was up there?" Maggie asked.

"A long time," Jonah deadpanned. "Your sister and Donovan just had their first baby a week ago. It was a boy," he told her with a totally straight face, although she couldn't turn around to see it. "They named him Jonah, after me."

That was when Maggie laughed. "You know, you had me going there for a second," she told him.

"Oh?" he asked innocently. He kept his head down, talking close to her ear so that she could hear him. "What gave me away?"

"Because after what we've just been through," she told him, almost shouting so that he could hear her and not have the wind whip her words away, "Bellamy wouldn't have gotten married without me there. Really," she asked more seriously, "how long have I been out here?"

He thought back to what Rae Lemmon had said to him. "By my best estimation, probably close to twenty-four hours."

That made sense, Maggie thought. "That would explain why I feel like I'm starving," she said. And then she ventured another look up at the sky. She almost wished she hadn't. "It looks like it's going to rain harder," she reported in dismay.

Without his hat to shield him, Jonah quickly glanced up and then looked down again. "That would be my guess," he concurred.

She looked straight ahead and had no idea where

they were going. She could hardly make out anything. The rain was obliterating everything around them.

"Are we going to get back to town in time?" she asked him anxiously.

That was easy enough for him to answer. "Nope, afraid not," Jonah replied simply.

That startled Maggie enough for her to attempt to twist around to get a better look at him. She nearly wound up sliding off the horse.

Jonah immediately tightened his arms around her again. "Didn't anyone ever teach you not to make any sudden moves when you're riding double in the middle of a storm?"

"Never had a need for anyone to point that out before," Maggie answered, feeling exasperated again. "If we're not headed to town, then where are we going?"

"Well, we definitely need shelter so we're going to the closest place I know of—if it's still standing," he qualified. He hadn't checked on it since Hurricane Brooke had paid the area this unexpected visit.

He could feel Maggie growing antsy. "My place," he told her. "It's a one-room cabin, but right now, it's probably our best bet if we want to wait out this newest wave of Hurricane Brooke," he said.

As he answered her question, Jonah shifted ever so slightly so that he could pull the ends of his slicker apart. The second he did that, Jonah carefully tucked the two sides around the woman sitting directly in front of him.

"It's not much," he granted, "but at least it'll give you some protection against this rain."

"I'm already soaked," she told him. "But thank you," she added in a politer tone. Then, turning her face toward him—carefully this time so she wouldn't slid off—Maggie added, "And thank you for coming out to look for me."

"Hey, no big deal." Jonah shrugged off her thanks. "As it turns out, I just happened to be in the neighborhood," he cracked.

Maggie knew the man behind her had said something, but because the wind had increased, whipping his voice away, she hadn't been able to hear him. "What?" she practically yelled.

Jonah started to repeat what he'd said, then gave up. Instead, he just shrugged. "Never mind."

He didn't think she heard that, either. Right now, it felt as if the wind was scattering his words to the four corners of the earth before they could be heard.

Leaning in over the woman he was holding tightly against his chest, afraid she would slide off if he loosened his grip even just a little bit, Jonah raised his voice and yelled, "We'll talk later."

She nodded, not bothering to try to answer him.

Maggie kept her face forward, searching the area for a sign of something that resembled a building or anywhere that they could take shelter until this latest onslaught of rain finally passed. There was nothing.

She had never felt this dismally wet and cold—and hungry—before.

Finally, just as she was about to give up all hope,

she thought she could make out what looked to be a small cabin up ahead. For a second she fought the impulse to turn around and ask her white knight if what she saw was indeed his cabin. But considering the fact that her words would probably be lost before he even had a chance to hear them, Maggie decided that it would be in her best interest to just be patient and see if this was the actual final destination.

At this point, Maggie was grateful for any place that could keep them even moderately dry. She wasn't picky.

When they came to a stop, Maggie saw that they were right in front of the cabin. Up close, it looked less rustic and more modern, but as long as it kept them dry, that was all that mattered.

Maggie could feel her white knight dismounting. She was right—this *was* their destination. At least until the storm had passed.

Holding on to Cody's reins, Jonah faced her, waiting. "Need any help dismounting?" he offered.

She looked at him as if she debated whether or not to be offended.

"I'm Texas born and bred, so no," she replied. The next second, she got off the horse as gracefully as possible. But when her feet hit the ground, she found that her legs were a lot less sturdy than she'd thought. The honest truth was they were downright wobbly, and she almost sank straight down to the ground.

And she would have if he hadn't caught both her arms in an attempt to steady her.

"Careful," Jonah cautioned.

Embarrassed, Maggie murmured a stricken, "Sorry about that."

"Nothing to be sorry about. You spent a day up a tree. You're lucky you still remember how to walk," Jonah told her.

She took one tentative step only to find that her legs still insisted on buckling rather than supporting her.

"Not so sure I do," she admitted.

There was a part of him that couldn't believe he was actually holding Maggie Reeves like this, the way he had once dreamed of doing. Usually, dreams had a way of not measuring up to long-cherished expectations. However, in this case, holding Maggie Reeves against him was everything he had thought it would be—and more.

Her heart was doing a glorious, uninhibited dance in her chest and just for one wild moment, Maggie thought that Jonah was going to kiss her.

She could feel her breath all but backing up in her throat, held perfectly still by sheer anticipation. She wasn't sure but she thought she might have even leaned in a little to offer him a better target.

And then nature interfered.

*Again.*

"The wind's picking up again," Jonah told her, pulling his head back. "We'd better get inside before it gets any worse."

Maggie nodded, knowing that he was right and

that in all likelihood, the weather had just stopped her from making a huge mistake.

She told herself that she was relieved but wasn't altogether sure if she was.

# Chapter 3

In contrast with the chaos that was going on directly outside, the moment that Maggie walked into the cabin, she was struck by its strong, clean lines. There were no unnecessary extras visible anywhere, nothing personal that pointed to the man who lived here whenever he was in town. It could have been a rustic hotel room waiting for someone to come and inhabit it. And at least for now, it had been spared by both the hurricane and the ensuing flood that had come in its wake.

If there was any detraction at all, it was that very little light came into the cabin.

"I don't suppose the lights are working," Maggie said. To test her theory, she hit the switch by the door. Nothing happened when she did. "Apparently not," Maggie said with a resigned sigh.

Jonah looked up at the living area's vaulted ceiling. "At least the roof is intact and not leaking," he told her.

"There is that," she agreed with a smile as she glanced up.

Jonah made his way over to the gray flagstone fireplace. "I'll get a fire going. That should warm us up a little." He turned toward Maggie. His eyes slid up and down the woman and for the first time since he'd finally managed to locate her, he realized that she was drenched and dripping. "Why don't you go look in the bedroom closet and see if you can find something to change into?"

Almost self-consciously, Maggie glanced down at herself. There was a pool of water forming on the wooden floor just around her feet. She looked up again.

"What about you?" she asked.

"I'll change my clothes, too. But first I have to go back out and put Cody up for the time being." He could see she was about to ask him where he planned to put the horse. There was no barn on the premises. "The shed behind the house is still up."

"That's a piece of luck," she remarked.

"Yeah," he agreed with a laugh. "Otherwise, I'd have to bring Cody in here with us." He saw the surprised look on Maggie's face. The way he saw it, he wasn't suggesting anything *that* unusual. "I can't take a chance on losing our only means of transportation. Otherwise, we'll be stranded."

Made sense, she thought. "Need any help?"

Jonah sat back on his heels and watched as the bits of paper he had tucked in between the firewood began to burn. The flames spread, greedily consuming the wood that was all around them.

"No," Jonah answered, rising once he was sure that the fire in the hearth wasn't going to go out. "I got this covered. You just do what you need to do to get dry. The bedroom's back there," he added, pointing toward the rear of the cabin.

Not that it would have taken her an inordinate amount of time to find the room. The cabin consisted of the living area with a kitchenette on one side and a bedroom along with a three-quarter bath tucked directly behind the back of the fireplace.

Maggie looked after him uncertainly. "You sure you don't mind my rummaging through your closet?" she asked just as he crossed back to the front door.

Jonah smiled, surprised that she was standing on ceremony, given the unusual situation they found themselves in. "There're no skeletons in there if that's what you're worried about."

Maggie flushed slightly. "It's not that. I just thought that…"

Feeling awkward—after all, she didn't know the man *that* well—her voice trailed off, letting him fill in the blanks for himself.

"And you won't find anything in there to embarrass you—or me," he assured her. Turning up the collar of the all-but-useless rain slicker, he put his hand on the doorknob, turning it. "I'll be back as soon as I can," Jonah promised.

The next second, he pulled open the door and stepped out into the gusting rain.

Maggie hurried over to the front window to watch Jonah for as long as she could before he disappeared around the side of the cabin. From what she could see, it didn't look as if the hurricane was going to double back. With any luck, she thought, crossing her fingers, Brooke was done with them.

Now if the rain would just let up…

Backing away from the window, Maggie glanced down at the wooden floor she had just traversed. Her entire path was marked by drops of water.

"Time to stop leaving puddles," she murmured. "Guess I'll go see what he *does* have in his closet."

She'd thought that maybe Jonah would have some items of clothing that an old girlfriend had left behind—or perhaps even a current one. The way she saw it, it was more than possible. A man who looked like Jonah Colton couldn't be going through life un-attached for long, she reasoned. He was the kind of man that women literally threw themselves at.

But all she could find in the lone closet as well as in the tall chest of drawers were his clothes. Debating, Maggie finally decided to borrow one of his flannel shirts, but there was no way in the world that she was going to put on a pair of his jeans. Jonah Colton had a good eight inches or more on her, not to mention about eighty or so pounds—if not more. Any of his jeans that she would have put on would have come parachuting down.

She listened for a moment to make sure Jonah

hadn't come back, but only silence met her ears. Moving quickly she stripped off her utterly soaked shirt and put on one of the button-down work shirts from the closet.

Just as she thought, it fit her like a tent. She tied the ends together to make it nominally shorter.

Even so, it was way too big for her. It felt roomy enough for two of her to fit into the shirt.

Maggie had just finished assessing herself in front of the freestanding large mirror when she heard the front door open and then close again. Holding her breath, she hurried out to make sure that the person she heard was Jonah and not someone who had stumbled upon the cabin while looking for some shelter from the storm.

She released her breath when she saw it was Jonah.

"Is your horse all tucked away and dry for the time being?" Maggie asked as she joined Jonah in the main room.

"For now." His eyes swept over her. He did his best not to laugh. "I see you found something to wear—sort of," he tagged on, his eyes sweeping over her. "And you kept on your jeans," he realized. "Why?" Jonah asked, tossing off the rain slicker and heading for his bedroom.

"Well, decency is the first reason that comes to mind," she answered. "You and I aren't anywhere near the same size and while I can get away with sporting a pup tent as a shirt, there's no way I could wear a pair of your jeans without constantly worrying that I was about to wind up executing a pratfall."

"Point taken," he answered, his voice floating in from the back where he had disappeared. "Wow," he cried, "it feels good to peel off these wet clothes." He seemed only half-aware that she was there.

He might only be half-aware of her but that definitely was not her problem, Maggie thought. To say the least, she was exceedingly aware of *his* presence. So much so that she was trying hard *not* to envision the way he looked right now, standing in his bedroom, bare chested and who knew what else was bare—trying to decide what to put on to replace his wet clothes.

"You know," he said as he came out, startling her, "I do have a belt that I can lend you. It would help to keep my jeans up for you," he offered.

She couldn't help staring at his waist. Flat and muscular, her guess was that his belt would still be way too big to her.

"You might not have noticed," she told him, "but I'm a lot smaller than you are."

"Oh, I noticed, all right," he assured her.

Jonah had become keenly aware of every single inch of Maggie years ago, long before this hurricane had hit. He'd noticed her when he had still been an ugly duckling and she had been a swan. And she was right. Her waist was way smaller than his. He thought of a solution.

"I have a length of rope you could use around here somewhere," he said, looking about the living area.

"That's okay," she told him, waving away his suggestion. "They're practically dry."

"Liar," he teased. But he wasn't about to push this. Jonah rolled up his sleeves one at a time. "You said you were hungry."

Her eyes were drawn to his muscular forearms, and she remembered the way his arms had felt around her. Belatedly, she realized that he was probably waiting for her to answer.

"Starved," she told him, still looking down at his forearms.

He rummaged through the pantry that was right next to his refrigerator. "I'm afraid all I can offer you is either a box of sugarcoated cornflakes, or half a loaf of bread. Anything else—if I had it—would require a stove and electricity to make it edible."

Turning toward her, he held out the box of cornflakes in one hand and the loaf of bread in the other.

"Both," she said without any hesitation. "I don't remember the last time I ate." Her stomach rumbled as if on cue. She flushed as she glanced down, self-consciously. "But obviously my stomach does."

"We've all been there," he said, glossing over her rumbling stomach to help her cover up her embarrassment. "Have at it," he told her, handing her the box of breakfast cereal and the partial loaf of bread.

Maggie accepted both. If this was all he had on hand, he obviously didn't believe in stuffing himself. "I see that gluttony isn't one of your vices."

Jonah laughed, appreciating that she had retained her sense of humor despite the situation she had endured.

"No, but curiosity is." And then Jonah became serious as he asked, "What the hell were you doing out there with a hurricane about to hit the area? You were taking an awful chance with your life."

Rather than make up an elaborate excuse, Maggie leveled with him. "To be honest, I forgot all about the hurricane. Besides, the weather bureau is usually wrong with its forecasts more than half the time, anyway."

He watched her go at the cornflakes as if they were going out of style. She wasn't kidding about being hungry.

"You forget about Bellamy and Donovan's wedding, too?"

"No, I didn't," she answered, a little indignant that he would think she was such a scatterbrain. "I just thought I'd have enough time to get to Live Oak Ranch and then get back. When I left for the ranch, the wedding was a day away."

He supposed she had a point. But he had another question. "And just what was so important at the ranch that you had to go right then?"

Maggie waited until she'd had consumed another handful of cornflakes before answering. "The answer to a riddle."

Jonah frowned. She wasn't being clear, he thought. Was that on purpose, or was she just as in the dark about her so-called "mission" as it sounded?

"What kind of a riddle?" he asked.

Rather than just give him another vague answer, Maggie leaned forward and pulled out the map she had hastily tucked into her back pocket just before the threat of being swept away by the rushing waters had her climbing up into the tree.

Then she told him the whole story, such as it was. "A couple of days ago, I got a letter from my attorney informing me that my former late father-in-law, Adam Corgan, had left instructions in his will to send this map and the note he wrote to me after he was dead."

Well, he could see why that had aroused her curiosity. It would have aroused his, as well.

"May I?" Jonah asked, nodding at the map and note in her hand.

Maggie held out the papers for him to take. "Sure, go right ahead."

Jonah read the note twice and was no more enlightened than he had been a minute ago.

"'The truth shall set Elliott Corgan free.'" He read out loud, then looked up at Maggie. His brow was furrowed. "What's that supposed to mean?"

Maggie shook her head. "I have no idea. I found the tree," she told him, indicating the map. "That was the one I was clinging to when you rescued me earlier today," she explained. "But I didn't find anything there that made what was in the note any clearer. To be totally honest, I have no idea why Mr. Corgan would have wanted me to have this, or what he was cryptically trying to tell me. None of it made any sense to me."

"It's suspicious, all right," Jonah agreed, frowning as he glanced at the note again. Something was off here, he thought. He could feel it in the pit of his stomach, like something solid that just sat there. "Maybe the police chief has some idea what your late father-in-law was trying to say," he suggested.

"Late *ex*-father-in-law," Maggie corrected. She wasn't related to any of those people anymore. Emotionally, she never had been.

The corners of his mouth curved slightly. "No love lost I take it."

"Adam was okay, I suppose," she told him charitably. "But James..." she said, referring to her ex-husband. "Well, that's another story."

"That makes this note you were sent even more suspicious," he said, waving the map and note.

She laughed dryly. "You won't get an argument from me."

He'd been watching her as Maggie made short work of the bread and cereal he'd given her. "Sorry I can't offer you anything more than just that bread and stale cereal," he apologized again.

"Right now, this is a feast," she assured him—and then suddenly she realized what she was doing. "And I'm hogging it all," Maggie said. She tilted the open box toward him. "Here, have some of your own cereal. There's not much left."

He held up his hand to keep her from pushing the box toward him. "That's okay, you eat it. I can wait until we get back to town."

*Town.* That sounded a million miles away, Maggie thought wistfully. "Is that going to be anytime soon?" she asked. "My sister must be worried sick about me."

Jonah laughed dryly. "Your sister is the reason I was out here looking for you in the first place. She was pretty scared now that you mention it. She was afraid that you might have drowned—or been blown away."

Maggie raised her chin defensively. "She should have known I can take care of myself," she said, doing her best not to let guilt overwhelm her. Her lips formed a pout. "You win a couple of beauty contests and everyone thinks you have cotton for brains and can't find your way out of a paper bag."

"I did find you up a tree," Jonah pointed out, trying not to smile.

"Right," she agreed. Then she said deliberately, "I was in a tree, I wasn't floating facedown in some storm-filled ditch."

"Well, if it means anything," Jonah told her quietly, "I never thought you had cotton for brains."

The unexpected affirmative comment caused Maggie to smile. "It means something," she replied. And then she stopped suddenly, cocking her head toward the window. "Hey, listen," she said, alert. "Hear that?"

Jonah did as she instructed. But, he thought, he obviously didn't hear what she did.

"Hear what?" he asked Maggie. "I don't hear anything."

"Exactly," she exclaimed, her eyes shining as she abandoned the empty cereal box on the scarred table and hurried toward the front window. She looked out, scanning the sky. "The storm's over," Maggie announced like a town crier. "Or at least it's stopped for now." She turned around to face him. "I think we should take advantage of the lull and get back to town before the weather decides to change its mind again."

"Best idea I've heard today," Jonah told her, although there was a part of him that would have liked to have lingered in the cabin a bit longer.

Maggie was already at the door. "What are we waiting for?" she asked. She couldn't wait to get back to civilization.

"I need to put out the fire," Jonah told her. When she looked at him, her brow wrinkled in confusion, it occurred to him that she might have misunderstood what he was saying. "In the fireplace," he added. And then he proceeded to do just that.

"Oh." Maggie felt like an idiot. She thought he was referring to something she'd felt going on between them. "Of course," she murmured belatedly.

"You wait here while I saddle Cody up," Jonah told her. He could see that she wasn't the type who liked being left behind. "I'll hurry," he promised, closing the door behind him before Maggie had a chance to protest.

Or before he had a chance to act on the feelings that were bubbling up inside him.

# Chapter 4

Bellamy was helping a family of three settle into their temporary quarters because the hurricane had rendered part of their house unlivable when she happened to look in the general direction of the side entrance. She dropped the blanket she was holding and completely lost track of everything else.

"Oh my lord, he found her!" Bellamy cried. "He found her!"

Before any of the family she was helping could ask her who she was talking about, Bellamy was racing across the rec center, trying not to bump into any of the people or the cots that had been hastily arranged throughout the large room.

Bellamy descended on her sister with an enthusiasm that came straight out of their childhood.

Reaching Maggie, she threw her arms around her, hugging the somewhat-bedraggled younger woman for all that she was worth.

Donovan reached Jonah and Maggie while Bellamy was laughing and crying, all at the same time.

"It's you, it's really you!" she exclaimed, beside herself with joy. Part of her had been terrified that she'd lost Maggie to the hurricane.

"Yup, it's me," Maggie managed to get out.

Bellamy was squeezing her so hard it was difficult for Maggie to draw a breath, much less actually be able to say something intelligible.

"You have no idea how scared I was that I'd lost you," Bellamy cried. "And we'd just finally resolved all those things between us and had gotten back together." Still hugging Maggie, she looked over her sister's shoulder at Jonah, who was standing right behind Maggie. "Thank you!" she cried, tears sliding down her face as her eyes met Jonah's. "I don't know how to ever repay you for this."

"It's just all in a day's work," Jonah assured his future sister-in-law.

He hadn't searched for Maggie in order to be thanked or praised, he'd done it because for him there was no other choice. If he hadn't found Maggie, he would have still been out there, searching for her.

"Bell," Maggie all but squeaked. "I can't breathe," she protested because her sister was hugging her even harder.

"Oh, I'm sorry," Bellamy apologized self-consciously. She released Maggie and took a step back. "I was just so sure that I'd lost yo—" Bellamy stopped talking as she took a better look at her sister. "What are you wearing?" she cried in amazement as she looked at the work shirt that was hanging off her sister's upper torso, all but going down to her knees.

In the excitement, Maggie had temporarily forgotten all about the shirt she'd put on. Collecting herself, she glanced down. She could see why Bellamy had reacted the way that she had.

"Oh, this. It belongs to Jonah." Because that all but *begged* for a further explanation, she told her sister and Bellamy's fiancé, "My blouse was completely soaked so Jonah offered me one of his shirts so I could have something dry to wear."

Bellamy looked quizzically at her sister's savior. "You carry spare shirts with you?" she questioned, somewhat confused.

"No," Maggie interrupted, "I got the shirt from his closet when we stopped at his cabin."

This wasn't making anything clearer. If anything, it was making things even more obscure. Bellamy exchanged looks with her fiancé.

"You stopped at Jonah's cabin?" she asked Maggie, trying to get things perfectly clear in her mind.

Jonah could see this conversation was going somewhere that seemed destined to make Maggie uncomfortable. Rather than get more tangled up in an explanation, he waved his hand dismissively at all of it.

"Long story," he told Bellamy and his brother. "Maggie'll tell you all about it once things settle down a little around here." To him it was more important to see to the survivors than explain why Maggie'd had a wardrobe change.

The recreation center was completely packed now and the people who had either lost their houses to the hurricane or had their houses so severely damaged that they were deemed unlivable would have to stay here until other, more permanent arrangements could be made. But the lucky ones would be going home soon, Jonah thought.

However, that didn't mean that his job, as well as that of the other members of the team tasked with rescue efforts for the town, was over. Far from it. There was still a great deal to do.

But he wanted to do one more thing before turning his attention back to rescuing the residents of Whisperwood. Jonah wanted to get a second opinion on this so-called riddle that had all but sent Maggie to her death.

"Has anyone seen the police chief around recently?" he asked his brother and Bellamy.

"Chief Thompson?" Donovan asked, surprised that Jonah was looking for the man. "I just saw him. He brought a stranded couple to the rec center in the last hour." Donovan looked around the area. "There he is," he declared, spotting the chief halfway across the rec center. He pointed toward the man for Jonah's benefit.

Chief Archer Thompson picked that moment to look in their direction. Seeing that Donovan was pointing at him, the chief headed toward the group to see what he wanted.

Tall, lean, with an authoritative air about him and very few gray hairs despite being in his midsixties, the chief smiled warmly at Maggie as he approached the small group.

"I see you found Maggie," he said to Jonah. "Nice work. Are you all right?" the chief asked the young woman, politely making no reference to her unorthodox oversize attire.

Maggie nodded, appreciating the man's concern. "I am now."

Since she was back, safe and sound, the chief allowed himself to comment on her initial disappearance. "Fool notion, going out like that in a storm," he admonished her. "Didn't you listen to the weather report?"

"In my defense," Maggie told the police chief, "there was no storm when I left—and the weather bureau only gets things right a fraction of the time."

"Yes," he agreed. "But it *was* the day before your sister's wedding." He would have thought she would be busy helping her sister with the details for the wedding. "If you don't mind my asking, why were you out, running around the countryside like that?"

Jonah decided to step in. "That's what I wanted to talk to you about," he told the chief. He took out the map and the note that Maggie had given him. Glancing at Maggie to see if she had any objections about sharing this information with the chief—she apparently didn't—he handed both over to Thompson. "Maggie was looking into this."

Jonah saw the chief raise an eyebrow and in the

interest of brevity, he explained, "Adam Corgan left instructions in his will for the map and note to be sent to Maggie upon his death. We'd like to know what you make of it?"

All the chief needed was one glance at the map to tell him that he was looking at the Live Oak Ranch. The accompanying note, though, proved to be more of a mystery.

"'The truth shall set Elliot free.'" Thompson read, then looked up at Maggie and Jonah. "What truth?"

"To be honest, that was what we were hoping you might be able to tell us," Maggie confessed.

Thompson frowned, looking at the note again. It was just as obscure on the third reading as it had been on the first two.

"Well," he said slowly, "this obviously has something to do with Adam's older brother, Elliot."

"The one who up and disappeared years ago? Wasn't he rumored to be that serial killer?" Donovan asked. Everyone but the chief looked at him in surprise. For the most part, Donovan had just been listening to what the others were saying, but this had made him think back to the stories he'd heard shared from decades ago. "The one who killed those six young women? That was, what, forty years ago, wasn't it?"

Thompson suppressed a sigh. This had been hushed up by Corgan's family but after all this time, the chief saw no reason to keep it silent any longer.

"Exactly right," the chief said grimly.

Maggie felt totally bewildered. "He was a serial killer?" she cried.

"I'm afraid so. The Corgan family paid good money to have this covered up. But with Adam dead, this was bound to come out," the chief said.

Maggie looked at the note again. "What do you think it means?" she asked the chief.

The look on the chief's face grew grimmer. "It means that you should stay away from anything that has to do with this case." He glanced from Maggie to Jonah. Neither one looked as if they were in the least bit intimidated. "I'm serious, you two. I don't know what Adam had to have been thinking when he wrote this or why he would have wanted to pull you into this family mess after all this time. But I guess now we'll never know, since Adam's not going to be answering anyone's questions anymore."

"But maybe Elliot could," Jonah suddenly said, speaking up. If anyone should know what was behind this riddle, it would be the man the riddle specified by name. "Do you know where he is, Chief?"

"Yes," Thompson replied, making the decision to end his own silence. "He's in Randolph State Prison in Austin. Has been for forty years."

"Then he was convicted of killing all those women?" Jonah asked.

Stunned because she'd never known any of this when she was married to James, Maggie asked, "How was this not public news?"

"I told you. The family paid to keep this quiet," the chief said.

"That money they paid, did that include you?" Jonah asked.

"I had other reasons," Thompson answered without elaborating any further. He was long passed the point of getting annoyed by careless questions. "What's important is that Elliott was found guilty by a jury of his peers and he's been incarcerated for the last forty years," Thompson said quietly. "The bastard got what he deserved," the chief added with genuine feeling and finality. "I was serious before," he said to Maggie and Jonah. "I want you to stay away from this. There is no 'truth' to set Elliot free. He killed all those poor young women who, as far as was known, never did anything to him except to have the misfortune of crossing his path. The man needs to go on paying for his crimes."

As if on cue, the shortwave radio Thompson kept attached to his belt began to crackle, calling for his immediate attention.

He held up his hand to stop any further discussion. "I've got to take this," the chief said, addressing the small group.

So saying, Thompson removed the radio from his belt and walked away so he could speak to the person who was calling in private.

Maggie frowned, looking at the chief's back as the man walked away from them. "He's not telling us something."

"I'm sure Thompson's not telling us a lot of things," Jonah commented. He looked at the situation from the point of view of the job he'd been tasked with. "The man's got a lot on his mind right now, including roughly four dozen missing town residents—" He glanced down at Maggie. "One less of course, now that you're here."

"No." Maggie shook her head. "I meant he's not telling us everything about Elliot Corgan," she insisted. "Did you notice the look that came over his face when he said the man's name? I thought his jaw was clenched so hard it was going to snap."

"Well, he probably was one of the police officers on the case at the time," Jonah guessed. "The chief had to have had firsthand knowledge of all those killings and how they affected the victims' families. This note from beyond the grave from the guy's brother just brings it all back for him," Jonah speculated. "Combine that with what he's doing now and none of it can be easy for him."

Maggie hardly heard him. Instead, she suddenly recalled something. "Donovan said something about six victims."

Jonah looked at her, wondering where she was going with this. "So?"

"What if there were more than just six victims?" Maggie asked him. "All this was kept hushed up, right. Well, what if Elliott hadn't been forthcoming about the number of women he killed? What if this so-called 'truth' that Adam referred to in his note refers to more bodies?"

"How would finding them set Elliott free?" Jonah asked.

"I haven't figured that part out yet," she admitted.

"The chief told us to stay away from this," Jonah reminded Maggie. He looked at her face. He imagined that she had the same look when she went off to seek this so-called "truth" that Adam had urged her to unearth. "But you're not going to listen to him, are you?"

She turned toward Jonah. "I can't shake the feeling that I got that note for a reason. That this 'truth' I'm supposed to find has something to do with finding out if there's more to Elliott's killing spree than the chief knew about. If there are more bodies out there, their families deserve to know about it. They deserve closure instead of thinking the women just ran off."

"I agree," he told her. "But, again, how would that set Elliot free?"

She shrugged. "I don't know. It could be that Adam wasn't firing with all four cylinders," she guessed. "Maybe in Adam's mind, finding more bodies will somehow absolve Elliot of those murders. Maybe he *didn't* kill those women."

Jonah was studying her as Maggie talked about this. "You sound like this has really gotten to you," he observed.

She flushed a little, but she wasn't about to apologize or make excuses. "I guess it has."

Jonah hazarded a guess. "Is it because this is your ex-husband's family?"

She laughed dismissively. "If anything, that would be enough of a reason to make me keep my distance from trying to find an answer to this riddle. No, I'd have to say that this intrigues me," she confessed. "I hate unsolved mysteries and here's one right in my own backyard."

He nodded slowly, taking this all in. "So you're planning on looking into this even though the chief told you not to."

She didn't see it as being defiant. She looked at it from another point of view.

"You said yourself the chief's got his hands full. He can't be everywhere, which means he definitely can't take the time to look into this now and like I said, I feel like I owe it to the victims' families to find some answers."

He'd seen that stubborn expression on her face before, although only from a distance. This was the first time that he'd been so close to it. The woman was gorgeous when she had her mind made up.

"So you're going to go ahead with this investigation no matter what I say," Jonah concluded.

Maggie raised her eyes to his and asked, "What do you think?"

"Honestly?" he asked. Maggie nodded. "I think you're going to need a keeper."

She took offense at his words. "Look, you rescued me, and I know I owe you a great deal, Jonah. Maybe even my life, but that doesn't give you the right to order me around."

He cocked his head, confused at her interpretation. "I didn't say that."

Was he trying to backtrack? "You said I need a keeper," she reminded him.

"Yes, I did," he agreed. "The last time I looked, what a keeper does is keep track of whatever or whoever he's 'keeping.' In my book, that means that if you decide to play detective—"

"When," Maggie corrected.

Jonah continued as if she hadn't interrupted him, "You can't go running off on your own. You'll need backup."

Maggie had to admit—albeit silently—that she liked the idea that Jonah would be there with her to help if she needed it—which she willingly admitted that she very well might. The man was the very definition of capability—not to mention exceedingly easy on the eyes. If Jonah could find her in the aftermath of a hurricane and with floodwaters threatening to rise again, she had a feeling he would be invaluable in her search to discover if there were any more victims and why their bodies had never been recovered.

*A lot of questions and no direct path to an answer*, Maggie thought.

"Are you suggesting we form a partnership?" she asked Jonah.

Jonah didn't answer her immediately. Maggie was an ex-model and beauty contest winner who now taught etiquette and deportment lessons in her apartment, while he was part of Cowboy Heroes, a search and rescue team that did a great deal of their rescuing on the back of a horse. He was also a trained EMT.

They were as diverse and different in their approach to life as night and day, and the only thing they really had in common was that his brother was marrying her sister. But for whatever reason, Maggie was leaving herself open to accepting his help. There was *no* way he was going to tell her no. Somehow, he just had to get Maggie to hold off until he could be there for her. He did have people to rescue.

"In a manner of speaking," he finally said. And then he decided to be direct with her. "Listen, those other victims—if they do exist—aren't going anywhere and Adam Corgan sure as hell isn't, either. Why don't you give me a couple of days, maybe help me to coordinate rescue efforts for the town, and after that, I'm all yours?"

*All hers.*

The man had no idea how tempting that sounded, Maggie thought.

Before her imagination could take off, she roused herself and asked, "You want me to help you?"

"Not just me," he corrected. "You'll be helping the town."

Maggie smiled. He'd said just the right thing to get her attention. She had always wanted to give back to the community, to be seen as something more than just a pretty face. Mannequins had pretty faces, and no one thought highly of them—or at all, she thought. This, at least, was something meaningful and productive. Jonah was right. Adam and his riddle could certainly wait a few more days.

"Sure," she told Jonah. "Count me in. I'd be more than happy to help with the rescue efforts," she said with a warm grin, "seeing as how I have firsthand experience with what it feels like to be rescued."

"Then, if you're feeling up to it," he qualified, "let's get started."

"Absolutely," she responded, following him out the door. "Let's."

## Chapter 5

Jonah slanted a look toward Maggie. She was holding up a lot better than he had thought she would, considering the fact that this morning he'd found her stuck up in a tree. Anyone else would have easily milked that experience and placed themselves out of commission for at least a couple of days, if not more.

But she hadn't. Maggie had insisted on coming out with him to help with the search and rescue efforts.

There was no doubt about it. Maggie Reeves was one tough lady. Somehow, although she wasn't trained for it, she'd managed to keep up with him all day. She spent most of that time helping him find survivors, digging them out whenever that was necessary. Overall, what the survivors they found needed most was to be comforted and that, he quickly realized, seemed to be Maggie's specialty. She was kind and comforting, able to quiet children when they cried, and on occasion, she could even make them laugh.

All in all, she was a great asset.

It was getting dark when he finally came up to her and said they were calling it a day for now.

"Are you sure?" she asked, even though she felt more drained and exhausted than she ever had before in her life. "There're more people out there," she protested. Not to mention that there was still a little bit of daylight left.

"Yes," he agreed, "and there are also more people than just the two of us to help find them." Jonah smiled at her and without thinking, he wrapped one arm about her shoulders, gently guiding her away from the pile of sticks and plaster that just a short while ago represented someone's house. "You did good today. Better than good," he amended. "But I definitely think that it's time you went home. C'mon," Jonah gently urged, "I'll take you." When he saw Maggie open her mouth, he knew what was coming. Jonah was quick to put a stop to any protest. "Don't argue. I'm the leader."

Maggie laughed softly, shaking her head in surprise. "I thought this was a partnership."

"It is," he assured her. "But I'm still the leader. That means you have to listen to me. Let's go," he prodded politely, leaving no room for argument.

Because he had stabled Cody earlier in the day, Jonah was driving his pickup truck now. After getting in, he fastened his seat belt and waited for Maggie to get in on the passenger side. He knew where she lived, but he waited for her to give him her address.

Over the years, for one reason or another, he had inadvertently found out a great many things about Maggie. He had taken an interest in her life. However, he knew how that would sound to someone else— or to Maggie herself if she knew. The last thing he wanted was for her to think he was stalking her, even though in this instance the only reason he knew where she lived was because Donovan had mentioned it to him when his brother and Bellamy had been putting their wedding together.

"Okay, direct me," he told her, waiting. "Where do I go?"

The second Maggie sank down in her seat, she felt instantly exhausted. Rousing herself, she mumbled the address to Jonah. She lived in an apartment located within a collection of buildings that had been whimsically named Whisperwood Towers.

"Whisperwood Towers, here we come," Jonah announced, turning the key in his ignition. His pickup truck rumbled to life.

As he drove to the Towers, he spared a glance in Maggie's direction. Her head was definitely beginning to droop.

"Why don't you get some shut-eye?" he suggested. "You've earned it. I'll wake you up when we get there."

"I'm fine," she told Jonah even as her eyelids were shutting on her.

A few minutes later, Jonah smiled to himself as he

listened to her even breathing. "Yup, I can see that," he murmured quietly, amused.

But Jonah's amusement vanished as he approached the site of Whisperwood Towers—or where the apartment buildings were supposed to be.

The structures were no longer standing tall and erect. The Towers had received the brunt of the hurricane's assault as Brooke passed through the town. In more than three-quarters of the buildings, there was rubble where the walls had once been.

"Damn," Jonah swore under his breath. Adjusting the rearview mirror, he carefully tried to pick his way back out. Without meaning to, he rolled over something large in the road.

The sudden thrusting movement had Maggie waking up with a start.

The first thing she noticed was that the pickup was moving backward. She looked at Jonah. "Why are you heading away from the apartment buildings?" she asked. And then, only because there was a full moon out, she saw the reason why he had suddenly reversed his direction. Her eyes widened in shock. "Omigod, is that…?"

Jonah really wished he could tell Maggie that she was looking at something else, but he wasn't about to insult her with a lie. Maggie could see for herself the remnants of Whisperwood Towers—the place that she had been calling home even before her divorce had been finalized.

"I'm afraid so," Jonah said, answering her unfinished question.

Stunned, Maggie felt her throat closing. Everything she had ever called her own was in that demolished apartment. She could only stare at what was left of the towers and say the words that so many others had either thought or said out loud in the last couple of days. "I have no place to stay."

Jonah never hesitated. "Yes, you do," Jonah informed her, his tone leaving no room for Maggie to mount an argument. "You're staying with me."

Still staring at the Towers remains, which were now growing smaller and smaller as Jonah drove them away from the scene, Maggie needed more than a second to absorb his words.

When she did, Maggie shook her head. "That's very generous of you, but I can't take you up on your offer," she protested.

He hadn't expected this to be easy. He had a feeling that it was her damn pride that was making her say that. "Why not?"

Maggie's mind jumped to the first logical excuse that came to her. "Well, because there's only one bedroom in your place," she pointed out.

He wasn't about to let her refuse. "I know you're a gorgeous ex-beauty queen, but I promise I'll find a way to restrain myself," Jonah told her. And then, more seriously, he said, "We're two adults, Maggie, who are in the same dire situation everyone else around here seems to find themselves in. I'll take the couch and you can have the bed. There's a lock on the bedroom door. You can use it if it'll make you feel any better," he added.

"I trust you," she told him, ashamed that she had instantly thought of Jonah behaving just like James would have in the same circumstances.

Jonah wasn't anything like James. To begin with, James would never have been out there, trying to find survivors and rescuing them. James had never done a selfless thing in his life.

"Good," Jonah replied, doing his best to keep a straight face as he told her, "and I trust you."

"Me?" Maggie questioned incredulously.

"Sure. Why, you never heard of a woman having her way with a man?" he asked her, struggling to maintain his straight face.

Gripping the steering wheel, Jonah stared straight ahead. The full moon and his headlights provided the only illumination for the pitch-black road in front of them. Lucky for him he could find his way to his family's ranch even if he were blindfolded.

Jonah had sounded so serious when he asked the question, Maggie had to laugh. After everything she had gone through today, she'd thought that she would never be able to laugh again.

It really felt good to laugh. She silently blessed Jonah for that.

"I promise I won't have my way with you," Maggie told him when she finally stopped laughing.

Humor curved his lips. "Just so you know, I won't hold you to that," he told her with a wink. And then he grew serious again. "I'm really sorry about your place, Maggie."

A sigh escaped her lips before she could suppress it. "Yeah, me, too."

"I've got an idea. Why don't we swing by come morning and take a look at the damage?" Jonah suggested. "Maybe it's not as bad as it looks right now in the dark."

She knew that Jonah was just saying that for her benefit. He was only trying to make her feel better.

"Maybe," Maggie murmured only out of a sense of obligation. She pressed her lips together. "I guess that was pretty egotistical of me, thinking that my place could have been spared after so many other places in town weren't."

"Not egotistical," Jonah said, correcting her. He had another word for it. "Human. Everybody undoubtedly hoped that their home had been spared because a few of the other homes and places of business had been." He really felt for her and tried to comfort her the way she had offered comfort to the rescued survivors today. "There's no rhyme or reason to what a hurricane does, why one building is either totally wrecked or pulled off its foundation and the one right next to it is totally bypassed and spared. It just happens," he concluded with resignation. "You can't drive yourself crazy wondering why. There's no real answer to that question."

She didn't know about that. "If I'd been home instead of out there, trying to unravel Adam's damn puzzle—"

She didn't have to finish. He knew what she was thinking. And he didn't want her dwelling on it.

He pointed out why. "You might have been like

Dorothy in *The Wizard of Oz* and gotten transported to another place."

Maggie could feel the tension beginning to leave her shoulders. She laughed. "That is really sugarcoating it," she told him.

"Hey," Jonah said, pretending to balk at her assessment of what he had said. "It's been a long day. Humor me."

She knew Jonah wasn't actually asking her to humor him, he was attempting to humor *her*. Or to at least soften the blow of what had just happened to her place and not allow her mind to dwell on a far more serious, unsettling scenario.

Maggie changed the subject. "You know, you don't have anything to eat at your place," she reminded Jonah. "I cleaned out your cereal."

"But we still have what's left of the bread," he teased her. Because he didn't want her contemplating going to bed hungry, he quickly rectified the image that she might be contemplating. "Don't worry, there's food. I asked one of the guys on the team to swing by the General Store—one of the places that hadn't been demolished by the hurricane—and pick up a few things. He brought them over to my place."

He smiled at her, trying to keep the situation light. "It was either that or come home after a grueling long day and start gnawing on the wood. I hear splinters are really bad for your digestion."

"You're trying to make me feel better about eating all your cereal, aren't you?" Maggie asked, smiling at him.

"Trying my damnedest. How'm I doing?"

Maggie deadpanned. "That depends on what that friend of yours managed to pick up at the General Store."

"Well, we're here," Jonah declared, pulling his truck up right in front of the cabin. "Why don't we go in and find out?"

After the chaos and destruction she had witnessed today, his cabin seemed even more like a haven to her than it had previously.

The Colton family's ranch was comprised of a thousand acres. Jonah's cabin was nestled in one corner of it, removed yet still very much a part of the whole general property.

This time, when Jonah walked in and threw the switch that was right by the front door, light permeated the interior of the cabin.

"What happened?" Maggie asked, looking around in surprise. "Was the power suddenly restored while we were driving over here?"

"Our power was," Jonah explained. "My family keeps a generator on the property. It had to be started up, but once it is, we're no longer at the mercy of the downed power lines throughout the surrounding area. This is no doubt thanks to the generator."

She turned toward the kitchenette. "If you've got a working generator, does that mean that the stove works, too?"

"Absolutely," he answered.

"And the refrigerator?" she asked, not wanting to take anything for granted.

"And the refrigerator," he echoed with a grin.

"Oh good. So let's see what your friend wound up getting for you."

Pulling open the refrigerator door, Maggie quickly took inventory of what was on the shelves. There was a carton of eggs, another loaf of bread and a package of bacon.

Maggie felt as if she'd just crossed into paradise.

"I see your friend is a great believer in breakfast being the most important meal of the day," she commented with a laugh.

She moved the newly purchased items around to see if they were blocking her view of anything else more substantial in the refrigerator.

They weren't.

Jonah had a feeling she had been hoping for more than just breakfast food.

"That's probably all that Jack could get for now," he said, referring to his friend by name. "The General Store is probably rationing their supplies, allowing customers to only buy a certain amount of items to insure that nobody goes hungry. Things'll get better once deliveries start being made again."

"I'm not complaining," Maggie assured him. "I like eggs better than I like cereal and I plowed through half a box of that today." She grinned ruefully. "I guess you can tell people I ate you out of house and home."

His eyes swept over her. "Not with that figure," he told her. "Nobody would ever believe me."

Maggie smiled at the compliment. It made her feel less grungy.

"Thanks. I needed that." She stifled an involuntary yawn, then looked at him ruefully. "I'm sorry. I guess I really am exhausted."

Jonah nodded understandingly. "Look, I'll just use the facilities and then you can have the bedroom so you can get to bed."

She had thought about that and had no intention of displacing him. "That's all right, Jonah. You don't have to be noble and give up your bedroom for me. I'm perfectly capable of taking the couch. Hey, I fell asleep in your car," she reminded him. "I can certainly sleep on the couch."

"This isn't up for debate," Jonah told her. "You'll sleep on the bed. Just give me a second," he said as he disappeared into the bedroom.

If he'd been alone, after the day he had put in, he would have taken a shower. But in the interest of letting Maggie get to bed, he skipped his shower and grabbed a change of clothes for tomorrow.

Coming back out, Jonah called, "It's all yours, Maggie."

When she made no response, he came into the main part of the cabin and looked at the couch. "Maggie?"

Coming closer, he saw the reason why she hadn't answered him. Maggie was totally out.

Jonah shook his head. "You had to have your way, didn't you? You are a damn stubborn woman, Maggie Reeves. But news flash, I can be stubborn, too," he said to the woman who was curled up on his couch, her head cradled in the crook of her arm.

He almost hated to disturb her, but he knew that she'd feel better in the morning if she didn't spend the night in such an awkward position.

Bending over, he slid his arm under her body and moving very slowly, he raised Maggie up from the sofa. Looking down at her face to see if he'd woken her up, he was satisfied that she was still asleep.

"Guess you were more tired than I thought," Jonah murmured.

Shifting her slowly, he began to head for the back of his cabin and his bedroom.

Maggie had nestled her face against his chest, and she made a noise now that sounded a little like a contented cat snuggling up for a nap. Jonah stopped walking for a moment, thinking that perhaps the motion might wake her up. But when she went on sleeping, he resumed making his way to his bedroom.

"Here you are, ma'am," he said quietly, reaching his bed. "Not exactly a palatial suite, but it's comfortable and you're welcome to use it for as long as you're here." Saying that, Jonah gently laid Maggie down on his bed.

He paused only long enough to remove Maggie's shoes and then to lightly cover her body with the ends of the bedspread that his mother had given him and insisted that he put to use.

Maggie Reeves, in his bed. Who would have ever thought it, he wondered, quietly looking at her sleeping face for a long moment.

"Sleep tight, Maggie," he whispered. "You've earned it."

And with that, Jonah tiptoed out of the bedroom and closed the door behind him.

## Chapter 6

The disorientation was immediate.

When Maggie opened her eyes the following morning, she had no idea where she was.

And then she remembered. The thought hit her like the sudden flash of a lightning bolt.

All her things were gone, destroyed because the building she had lived in had committed the sin of being in the path of a hurricane with the improbable gentle name of Brooke.

Throwing off the comforter that Maggie couldn't remember covering herself with, she sat up, blinking and trying to focus on her surroundings.

Daylight was creeping into the bedroom, making its way along the wooden floor. That told her that it had to be morning.

But how did she get here?

The last thing she remembered was leaning back against the sofa's cushion. She must have fallen asleep, Maggie thought. But that still didn't explain how she had gotten into this bed.

Wanting answers, Maggie slid off the bed. The second her feet hit the floor, she realized that she was barefoot. But she'd had on boots when she fell asleep, she was sure of it.

A quick search around the perimeter of the bed reunited Maggie with her boots. Try as she might, she couldn't remember taking them off. And if *Jonah* had removed them without waking her, then she must have *really* been out of it.

Her eyes suddenly widened as another thought occurred to her. Had he removed anything else from her person?

A quick check of what she was wearing—and if it had been disturbed in any way—told her that if Jonah *had* undressed her, he'd put everything back just the way he'd found it. That seemed highly unlikely.

Jonah wouldn't have tried to undress her, Maggie silently insisted. He'd taken the boots off—and left them off—purely for her comfort. But he'd obviously left everything else just the way he had found it. She had known Jonah Colton for most of her life—not intimately, but well enough to know that his character, as well as that of his brothers and parents, was exemplary.

Still, a tiny kernel of doubt nagged at her.

Well, there was only one way to find out, she told herself. She was just going to have to ask him.

Maggie headed toward the bedroom door and went to open it—just as Jonah presented himself on the other side of the door, about to knock. As a result, his raised hand came very close to making contact with her forehead.

It was hard to say which of them was more startled by the other's sudden appearance. They both jumped back before they could bump into one another.

"Sorry," Jonah apologized, dropping his hand to his side. "I was just coming to tell you that breakfast is ready."

Maggie didn't care about breakfast. She needed something cleared up first. "What was I doing in your bed?"

The question caught him off guard. "Sleeping would be my best guess."

Was he being flippant? "No, I mean how did I get there?"

He didn't understand why she looked so annoyed. "You fell asleep on the sofa, but you didn't look all that comfortable, so I carried you into the bedroom and put you in my bed," he concluded, thinking that would satisfy her.

"Anything else?" Maggie asked.

Jonah thought for a second, trying to recall if he had left anything out. "Well, I took your boots off because I thought your feet might start to hurt if you spent the night in them."

Maggie blew out a breath. Was he stalling? "What else?"

He looked at her as if he didn't understand what she was trying to get him to say. "I pulled the comforter over on you."

Maggie waited. When he didn't say anything further, she asked, "And that's all?"

Was there some ritual she had expected him to follow? "Why? What else was I supposed to do?"

Maybe she'd spent too many years with James and it had made her suspicious of all men. "Nothing," she answered, then hesitated. "But—"

He took that as her final answer. "Well then, I lived up to your expectations, didn't I?" Jonah concluded. "C'mon," he urged, "your breakfast is getting cold." Turning on his heel, he led the way back into the kitchenette. "I made coffee," he added, then warned her, "but there's no cream or sugar."

She usually liked to have both, but this wasn't the time to be choosy. "That's all right. I'll adjust," she said.

Biting her lower lip as she sat down at the small table and looked at the plate he'd prepared, she felt a little uncomfortable about the conversation that had transpired between them. The man had gone out of his way to be nice and she was interrogating him.

"I didn't mean to sound as if I was accusing you of something just now—" she began.

Another man might have enjoyed having her squirm through an apology, but that sort of behavior had never been Jonah's style. Thinking to spare her, he was quick to gloss over the incident.

"That's okay—I understand. You woke up in a different place than where you remembered falling asleep. The truth of it is we don't know each other all that well anymore." As he picked up his fork, he shrugged away the need for her apology. "You're a beautiful woman who's probably dealt with more than your share of overbearing Neanderthals who felt they were entitled to share more than just your company. It's only natural for you to have your imagination run away with you." Pausing before he began to eat, he looked into her eyes. "But I'm not a Neanderthal," he told her simply, "even though I was ready to climb into that tree to get you."

That completely broke the tension that was building between them. Relieved, Maggie laughed.

"So we're good?" he asked, taking a cue from her laughter.

"We're good," Maggie answered. "And so is breakfast," she added, looking down at her plate. She had almost finished half of it without even realizing it. "I never pictured you as being able to cook."

He didn't think that was much of a mystery. "Hey, considering the kind of life I lead, it was either learn how to cook or get really, really skinny. I decided to learn how to cook."

She nodded, trying not to be obvious about looking at him. "Good choice." She paused as she put another forkful into her mouth. It wound its way through her system, then down into her stomach. Maggie thought of what he had just told her. "So this is what you do for a living? You go around on your white horse, rescuing people?"

"Cody's a palomino," he corrected her. "And don't forget the search part," he said, amusement curving his mouth. There was also another part of his job. "I'm also trained in emergency medicine, but to answer your question in a nutshell—"

"Too late," she teased.

He didn't miss a beat. "Yes, this is pretty much what I do for a living. The organization's branch office is located in Austin. It's where I live," Jonah added.

That would explain why she hadn't seen that much of him these last few years, she thought.

"Well, lucky for me, you decided to come down for the wedding," Maggie told him.

He didn't want to take any undue credit. "Once the hurricane hit, headquarters would have sent my team out here to look for survivors one way or another."

Maggie shrugged away his attempt at modesty. "You look at it from your point of view, I'll look at it from mine."

Finished, she began to rise to bring both her plate and his to the sink.

"I'll do that," Jonah told her, quickly getting up from his chair.

She wasn't about to relinquish the plates, pulling them out of his reach "You cooked, I'll clean up. I like pulling my weight."

Jonah raised his hands up to indicate that he was withdrawing his claim to the dishes. "I didn't mean to imply that you didn't," he said. Smiling, he reminded her, "I saw you in action yesterday, remember?"

Maggie wasn't following him. "What does that mean?" she asked him.

He didn't want her getting all defensive on him again. They needed to progress past that point.

"It means that I know you can pull your own weight. Look, why don't we just agree that we're in this together?" he suggested. "That way you can stop circling around me, waiting for me to do or say something to challenge you. This isn't a contest, or a competition," he told her pointedly. "If you like, I can make you a temporary search and rescue team member. Will that make you feel better about this whole thing?"

People had a tendency, because of her looks, not to take her seriously. That Jonah just took her seriously without having her argue him into it felt as if she had just taken a huge step forward.

"I'd like that a lot," she replied. "What do I have to do?"

"Just what you've been doing since yesterday," he told her.

Maggie looked at him, waiting for more. When Jonah didn't say anything further, she asked, "And that's it?"

He smiled at her. "Trust me, that's more than enough," he assured her. "Okay, let's hit the road."

She was more than eager to go.

\* \* \*

The rest of the day was more or less a replay of the kind of work he and Maggie had undertaken the previous day.

Because Jonah was worried about how wandering around the rubble that had once been her apartment might affect Maggie, he made the decision that he and Maggie would concentrate their search and rescue efforts to another portion of Whisperwood.

For the most part, they helped coordinate the different rescue groups, deciding where each of the groups could be best utilized, depending on the nature of their skills.

However, Jonah knew that he couldn't put off having Maggie deal with whatever destruction had befallen her apartment indefinitely. So sometime in the midafternoon, he and Maggie made their way back to Whisperwood Towers. Or at least what was left of it.

Jonah could almost *feel* Maggie stiffening as she sat next to him in the truck. They were drawing closer to the site of what had once been the Towers.

Maggie shivered. "It looks worse in daylight," she said, the words coming out in a hushed whisper.

The building that she had lived in had been comprised of three floors. Her apartment had been located on the second floor. All three floors had come down, the first two floors crushed beneath the third.

"It looks like a deflated accordion," Maggie added under her breath, walking through the rubble. "I don't think there's anything from my apartment that I can even find. At least not in one piece." Blinking, she struggled to keep her tears from spilling. She refused to cry. Deep down inside she knew if she started to, she wasn't going to be able to stop. Turning toward Jonah, she said, "It's all gone."

"Maybe not," he told her, doing his best to bolster her spirit. "You'd be surprised what can turn up during the cleanup efforts."

"Don't," she said, a warning note entering her voice. "Don't pretend like you can hold out hope for me when there isn't any."

"I'm not pretending," Jonah insisted. "I've been at this a lot longer than you have and I've seen miracles, large and small, happen all the time, especially when you least expect it." He could see that Maggie refused to buy into his optimism. "I'll be sure to tell the cleanup team to sift through this area carefully rather than just bulldoze through it." But she remained impassive. "You might be surprised."

"Uh-huh, sure," Maggie answered, staring down at what might or might not have been part of her apartment. There was just too much rubble to be able to tell.

Jonah knew she didn't believe him, and in her place, he probably wouldn't have, either. But as he had told Maggie, he had seen things that she hadn't, so he was in a better position to hold on to hope, however slim the thread was.

"Do me a favor, Maggie," he requested.

The eyes that looked up at him were watery. He could see she was doing her best not to let what she saw get to her, but it seemed to be a battle that was destined to be lost—and soon.

"What?" Maggie asked, doing her best to regain her composure.

"Reserve judgment until all this is over," Jonah said.

"Fine," she sighed, forcing herself to think of something else. Anything but her apartment and the possessions that were in it. "Consider it reserved." Wanting desperately to change the subject and focus on something else, she turned the conversation around back to Jonah. "I've been meaning to ask, why aren't there any personal touches in your cabin?"

"It's very simple. Because I don't live there anymore," he answered. "I haven't really lived in the cabin for a few years. But whenever I'm home, I use it as a base."

"So where do you live?" Maggie asked. "I mean on a permanent basis."

He thought he'd already answered that. Maybe she hadn't understood. Given what she was going through, he couldn't fault her. "I live in Austin."

"Any particular reason?" she asked, curious. She knew why she had left—she was looking to help her family. But she had returned once she'd decided to divorce James and now she felt safe here as well as happy. She didn't understand why he would choose to leave Whisperwood when his whole family was here.

"I wanted to make a name for myself someplace where the name Colton doesn't instantly bring my father and his ranch to mind."

She thought of her own situation until recently. "Is there bad blood between you?" she questioned. She hadn't heard anything, but that didn't mean that all was rosy within the confines of the Colton family.

He was quick to set her straight. "Not at all, I just don't believe in hanging on to anyone's coattails." He smiled at her. "I prefer my own coattails."

"I guess I can understand that," she admitted.

For her, family had always been the source of pain and misunderstanding. She had married James with the best of intentions. Yes, in the beginning, she had been in love with him—James had been her high school sweetheart—but her marriage had quickly soured when she discovered that he was cheating on her. She'd married him because she loved him and because she wanted to use his money to help her parents, who had incurred a great deal of medical debt since they'd been involved in a car accident. Her love for James might have died, but her resolve to help her parents did not.

However, she wasn't able to get the money quickly enough. Both of her parents had died before she was able to pay off their debts. Not wanting to have anything to do with James's money once she was finally awarded it, she wound up using it to buy her sister the house where they had grown up.

Stunned, Bellamy was forced to reassess her feelings about and toward Maggie. She realized that when Maggie had gotten married and moved away, she was really doing it in order to help the family, not to escape dealing with the problems that nursing two invalids created. Once she realized that, all of Bellamy's bitterness vanished.

"Although," Maggie went on to tell Jonah, recalling her own situation, "sometimes it's nice to have family coattails to hang on to. You don't realize that until you suddenly find that there aren't any coattails for you to reach out for. That all you're grasping is air."

She really sounded as if she was in a bad way, Jonah thought. He hated to see her like this, hated what she had to be going through. He didn't want to pry, not yet, so he dealt with the situation another way.

"Why don't we knock off early?" he suggested. "Give you a chance to breathe, clear your head, forget about all this?" He gestured toward the rubble around them.

"It'll still be there to deal with tomorrow," Maggie said.

Then she understood what he was saying, Jonah thought. "Exactly. Tomorrow might be better."

But Maggie shook her head. "No, what I mean is we might as well make more headway today. That'll be that much less we all have to deal with tomorrow. And," she concluded, "we'll be one step closer to getting back on our feet."

Jonah studied her for a long moment, replaying her last words in his head. He had to admit that he was impressed. "Like I said yesterday, you are one tough cookie, Maggie Reeves."

"I don't know about tough," she told him. "But I'll

tell you this much." She squared her shoulders. "I certainly have no intentions of crumbling."

Jonah nodded, smiling at her. "Good for you. Okay, Maggie, let's get back to this while we still have some daylight."

He would get no argument from her.

# Chapter 7

A week went by and in the midst of all this chaos, Jonah found that he and Maggie had managed to forge a routine of sorts. Each morning they got up, had breakfast and then they joined the search and rescue efforts, trying to locate the residents who were still missing. They would spend the entire day digging, clearing and searching. At the end of the day, they would return to Jonah's cabin, almost too tired to chew.

To show their gratitude to the Cowboy Heroes, the owners of the General Store threw open their doors and generously provided provisions for all the volunteers involved in the search and rescue.

They also fed the volunteers who were clearing away the remnants of the houses that had been mostly blown down. The damage that had been sustained was just too great to repair. What was left in those cases had to be cleared away to allow new homes to rise out of the ashes, like the legendary phoenix.

Jonah noticed that Maggie was barely putting one foot in front of the other as they walked into his cabin at the end of another overly long day.

"Tired?" Jonah asked her.

She looked at him, wondering if he was trying to be funny. "I'd have to have a pulse to be tired. I think I'm beyond that," Maggie confessed. She sighed. It was an effort to form words. "And I am *so* beyond tired," she added with as much feeling as she could muster.

Because of the nature of what he did, Jonah was used to working like this. "You sit. I'll make dinner," he told her, gesturing toward the chair.

"That's not fair," she protested even as she practically fell into the chair, the absolute picture of exhaustion. "You made dinner last night. And the night before that. And the night before that."

She didn't think it was right that he had to do it again, although she couldn't summon the energy to get back up on her feet.

"You know," Jonah said, raising his voice as he took out a steak he intended to split between the two of them, "any other woman would be happy with this arrangement and accept it as her due without drawing this much attention to it."

"Well, I'm not any other woman," Maggie told him, meaning that, despite her exhaustion, she didn't think that this was her due or that taking advantage of him was fair.

Jonah laughed softly to himself. "You can say that again," he murmured under his breath.

He hadn't meant for her to hear that and she hadn't, at least not completely. But she'd caught enough to make her turn around to face him.

"How's that again?" Maggie asked.

Jonah debated saying something vague in reply, or simply telling her that he hadn't said anything. But instead, he turned up the heat under the frying pan, put the meat in the pan and said, "I certainly never thought that you were like any of the other girls when we were in school."

She stared at him, slightly bewildered. "You were five years ahead of me in school. I doubt you even noticed me."

The steak was sizzling and Jonah flipped it onto its other side. Was she actually serious? "*Everyone* noticed you," he told her simply. "Even before you hit high school, you were always too beautiful not to notice." He smiled, remembering the effect she'd had on him. "You were like an exquisite diamond in the middle of a basket filled with coals."

He'd said too much, Jonah thought. How had they even gotten to this subject? He had to learn not to say the first thing that came into his head.

He turned his attention back to the steak. Jonah knew that they both liked their steak rare, so frying it took next to no time at all. Done, he flipped the steak onto a plate, then cut it in half. He slid each piece onto a separate plate.

"Here," he said, placing the piece he had just cut in front of her and taking the remaining piece for himself. "Eat. If you're going to keep on arguing with me," he told Maggie, "you're going to need to keep up your strength."

She waited until she took the first bite. Damn, but that was good, she thought. "I wasn't arguing."

Jonah inclined his head, humoring her. "My mistake," he conceded.

She was tired, Maggie thought. Maybe she was being too touchy. "Telling a woman she's beautiful is never a mistake—unless you were just feeding her a line," Maggie said, just in case that was what he was doing.

"No line," Jonah assured her. "If you own a mirror, you'd know that." His eyes met hers. "You've always known that," he added. No one could be that oblivious to her looks.

When his eyes met hers, Maggie stopped eating. She was also fairly certain that for a minute, she'd stopped breathing, too. And just possibly, the world around them had stopped spinning.

The man sitting across from her was having a devastating effect on her.

"If *you* thought that," she said, "why didn't you ever say anything?"

He found that really amusing. "There was always such a crowd around you, I doubt you would have heard me," he replied.

Maggie frowned. "There was no crowd, Jonah."

He begged to differ. "You were one of the *really* popular girls. You were voted both the junior *and* the senior prom queen." And then he mentioned the biggest obstacle that kept him from making his feelings known. "Not to mention the fact that James Corgan was always there, ready to beat off any guy who came within two feet of you."

Maggie flushed when he mentioned her ex-husband. Having the man as part of her life wasn't something she liked being reminded of. But she couldn't dispute what Jonah was saying, either.

"He was my boyfriend at the time," she said, her eyes offering a silent apology for that part of her life and what had happened during that period.

"My point exactly," Jonah agreed. "I wasn't about to push my way in between the two of you. Not when you looked as if you had stars in your eyes whenever you looked at him."

Right now, it took everything for her not to shiver at the memory. "Maybe I didn't have stars in my eyes so much as I had sand in them," she corrected. When he looked at her, puzzled, Maggie explained, "I had sand in my eyes and I wasn't seeing clearly—or thinking clearly for that matter, either." Uncomfortable, she blocked out those memories. "Please, let's not talk about the past, Jonah."

He was more than happy to oblige.

"Fine with me," Jonah said. "If you don't mind, I'm going to grab a quick shower. I won't be too long," he promised. "And then you can have the bed."

Maggie gestured toward the back of the cabin. "It's your cabin," she reminded him.

"And you're my guest," Jonah countered. "That means I put your wishes ahead of mine."

Because of her marriage to James, she wasn't used to being treated with this much deference. "By all means," she told Jonah. "You take a shower."

"Five minutes," he promised, holding up all five fingers to underscore what he was saying as he crossed the room.

"Splurge," Maggie ordered. "Make it ten."

And then she found herself alone.

Maggie tried her best to keep her mind—and her hands—occupied as she waited for Jonah to come out again. But the moment he had closed the bedroom door behind him, tired as she was, her mind went into overtime, going to places that it had absolutely no business going.

Trying to rein in her thoughts, she reminded herself that even though circumstances had thrown them together again, circumstances would definitely pull them apart once this unusual epoch finally passed. Hadn't he told her that his life was in Austin, while hers, now that everything had been resolved, was finally back here.

Still, she just couldn't stop thinking about him or envisioning the way the water was probably lovingly cascading over and down that incredibly muscular body of his.

She forced herself to do something to occupy her mind.

Rinsing the dishes, she curled her hands into her palms, trying very hard not to picture him like that. So of course she did.

"All yours."

Stifling a squeal, Maggie swung around to see that Jonah was walking back into the living quarters, his hair still wet from the shower he'd taken.

Her hand covering her pounding heart, she told him, "You scared me."

"Sorry," he apologized, crossing to her. "I didn't mean to do that. I just thought that you'd want to get to bed as soon as possible so I came out the second I was finished taking my shower."

She felt her skin warming as his words evoked yet another image in her mind's eye.

Maggie pressed her lips together. "That's very thoughtful of you."

Trying to pass by him in what was rather a narrow space, she breathed in the scent of the soap Jonah had used. It was something manly and arousing—just like he was.

She tried to find her voice again. "But you didn't have to hurry on my account."

"Okay," Jonah replied, the words hanging between them as they stood so close to one another they were breathing in each other's air. Jonah could feel his pulse speeding up, rushing through his body as very strong desires swept through him, urging him to take her into his arms. "Next time I won't," he told her in a quiet voice.

His eyes, Maggie was sure, were saying other

things to her, things that had nothing to do with a shower. A warm shiver inched up her spine.

She didn't know why she was feeling so vulnerable right now, or what had triggered this reaction from her. Yes, they were both working side by side, but they were doing it as part of a whole.

However, at the end of the day they left together, and when they "came home," they occupied the same small space together.

Standing next to him now, she found herself almost willing Jonah to kiss her. She didn't think of it beyond that, didn't dwell on any of the consequences. All she knew was that, with her whole heart and soul, she really, really wanted Jonah to kiss her.

*And then what?* the voice in her head asked. Once the kiss happened, she would be opening up a whole can of worms, a can of worms she might not be capable of dealing with.

It was better not to go there and wonder than to kiss him and be disappointed. Although something told her that she wouldn't be disappointed.

Maggie was about to briskly tell him good-night when she felt the back of Jonah's long, tapering fingers brush along her cheek as he moved back a stray lock of her hair, lightly tucking it behind her ear,

Jonah was struggling to contain himself. Struggling not to give in to the urgent desire that was rushing through him as powerful as the river after the flood hit. He found himself being taken captive.

He desperately wanted to taste those lips of hers, to satisfy his mounting curiosity. But that in turn might ruin everything. They were getting along right now. If he gave in to the passions that were all but pounding urgent fists against the walls of his weakening restraint, he just might wind up regretting it.

Especially if he saw Maggie looking at him with disappointment in her eyes. Right now, they were friends, working together in total harmony. If he gave in to himself, all that could be lost.

He didn't want to chance it.

"You'd better get to bed," Jonah whispered, moving back. "We've got another long day ahead of us tomorrow."

She knew that, but wasn't he forgetting about something?

"What about the investigation?" Maggie asked, forcing the words out of her mouth. He'd told her that they would get back to it, but several days had passed and they still hadn't.

"Investigation?" he repeated, his mind still focused on how very tempting her lips looked and how much he wanted to kiss her.

"Into seeing if there were any more victims buried around that big oak," she explained patiently. Why else had her ex-father-in-law sent her that cryptic note if it wasn't to try to find other bodies?

The serial killer had left his victims buried in shallow graves, with barely just enough dirt thrown over their bodies. Other bodies would have surfaced by now—if he had buried them that way. But what if he hadn't? What if Elliott had decided to change his MO? Or what if there had been a copycat killer? Someone who had wanted to put his own signature on his victims?

What if *that* killer was the *real* killer and Elliott wasn't guilty at all?

Maggie wanted answers.

"You said that once the search and rescue had gotten underway, we'd go back to Live Oak Ranch together, to search around that tree that Adam marked off on his map," she reminded Jonah.

He nodded. "I remember."

He should have known that Maggie wouldn't forget about that. She had already proven to him that she was far too tenacious to allow the matter to drop no matter how busy she got. Or what the chief had said to both of them to get them to drop the investigation. It was obviously front and center on her mind.

"So when can we go?" she asked Jonah, her eagerness at war with the very tired look on her face.

"Tell you what," Jonah suggested. "We get everyone organized and going at the next search site tomorrow, and then the two of us can take a trip over to the Corgan ranch."

"To follow the map?" Maggie asked.

He knew better than to laugh at the eagerness he detected in her voice.

"To follow the map," he told her. "Maybe between the two of us, we can find whatever it was that Adam was trying to direct your attention toward." He thought back to the cryptic note she had shown him.

The one her late ex-father-in-law had left her along with the map. "It would have been nice if he hadn't resorted to riddles and just told you outright what it was he wanted you to find out there and just where you were going be able to find it."

She agreed that would have made it so much easier, but at least they did have something to go on.

"Look, I'm surprised that James's father even tried to reach out to me. I don't think, in all the time that I was married to James, that his father and I had any sort of a conversation that lasted for more than a couple of minutes and was about anything that went deeper than just speculating about the weather."

"And then he suddenly decides to put *this* on your shoulders?" He shook his head. It just didn't make any sense. "That is definitely a mystery," he agreed. Pointing toward the door right behind her, he ordered, "Go. Get to bed."

Maggie laughed, taking no offense. Every bone in her body wanted to do as Jonah instructed. "You are going to make one hell of a father someday," she told him.

He grinned at the thought. "I certainly hope so," he freely admitted.

Exhausted though she was, his response caught her off guard. "You want kids?"

"Absolutely," he said without any hesitation. "Two of each." And then he reconsidered his answer. "No, make that four of each."

"Four of each," she repeated, overwhelmed by the

thought of that many offspring. "You trying to lose your wife in the crowd?"

"No way. My parents had five of us and nobody ever got lost in that crowd," Jonah told her in complete sincerity.

*To each his own,* Maggie thought. His family apparently had much better luck with kids. Hers, it seemed, hadn't. Relations had broken down between her and her parents as well as between her and her sister. That had been a painful thing for her to endure. She didn't know if she was up to rolling the dice on having kids and risking that sort of rejection, not again.

"Okay," she declared as if that closed the subject they were discussing, however peripherally. "I'll see you in the morning."

"Right," Jonah agreed genially. "You'd better go get some sleep before we wind up finding something else to talk about."

She nodded, retreating and going into the bedroom. Maggie had a feeling that if she didn't, Jonah would be proven right. The man was easy to talk to and they *would* continue to find things to talk about. If that happened, before they knew it, it would be morning.

Being groggy and going out to be part of the search and rescue team was nothing if not completely counterproductive. In that state, someone would probably wind up having to rescue *them.*

Squaring her shoulders, Maggie told him, "Good night."

Jonah echoed the words back to her, the sound of his voice wrapping itself around Maggie, whispering a promise that was guaranteed to keep her warm until morning.

Maybe longer.

# Chapter 8

Jonah, Maggie happily discovered, was a man of his word. The moment he had finished overseeing the co-ordination of the day's rescue efforts and made sure that there were no new, unexpected emergencies festering in the wings, about to spring up, he turned toward her and said, "How do you feel about taking a ride out to Live Oak Ranch?"

Maggie had thought it was going to take him a lot longer before he said they could go. His question had caught her completely by surprise.

"Now?" she asked.

"Yes, unless you'd rather stay here and continue helping plow through all this dirt and rubble," Jonah answered, gesturing around the chaotic area. They had made a great deal of headway, but they weren't out of the woods yet. Not by a long shot.

"No, no," she quickly assured him.

She knew that it was work that needed to be done and she was more than willing to help. But Maggie also had this deep sense of urgency that was all but twisting her insides into a knot, an urgency that made her feel she was on the brink of solving a puzzle that was bigger than she was given to believe.

"Now is good," she told Jonah. Then she amended, "Now is perfect."

"Then 'now' it is," he responded, amused by her excitement as he led her over to his truck.

Trying to contain herself, Maggie climbed into the pickup truck. The moment she did, Jonah started the truck and they were on their way.

They traveled for over ten minutes and, at first, Maggie didn't say anything because she thought that maybe she had somehow gotten turned around during the search and rescue excursion this morning. She wasn't one of those people who was blessed with a powerful sense of direction that allowed her to find her way around even if she was moving in utter darkness.

But after another few minutes had gone by, Maggie became increasingly convinced that she *wasn't* mistaken. Jonah was driving them back into town, the completely opposite direction from Live Oak Ranch.

This wasn't making any sense to her. She shifted in the front seat to look at him.

"I thought you said we were going to Live Oak Ranch," she said.

Jonah continued driving, keeping his eyes on the road. "We are."

"No, we're not," she argued. "You're driving back into Whisperwood," she pointed out. Didn't Jonah see that?

"I know," he answered, his voice calm. "That's where the horses are."

"The horses?" she questioned, feeling increasingly lost. Had she missed something?

"Sure," Jonah answered as if the reply was as plain as the nose on her face. "If we're heading back to look around that tree you were clinging to when I happened by to rescue you," he reminded her, still teasing her about the incident, "that's some pretty rough terrain. We'll make a lot better time getting there if we go on horseback."

She blew out a breath. "Said the man who was practically born on the back of a horse."

He laughed at the "voice-over" Maggie had just used to illustrate her objection to his idea. He wasn't buying it. "This is Texas," Jonah reminded her. "Everyone was born on the back of a horse."

Obviously, he didn't see the problem. "Not everyone," she argued.

The road ahead was mercifully unobstructed so he could afford to look at her for a moment. Maggie had caught him completely by surprise. "You can't ride a horse?"

She didn't like the way that sounded. As if she was deficient in some way.

"I can get on a horse without falling off," Maggie said defensively. Then she added, "Although it is kind of tricky." She cleared her throat, looking straight ahead. "Most of the time I find another way to get from place to place—like using a four-wheel drive vehicle."

"Horses are better when it comes to getting around on terrain that's inhospitable." In his opinion, that only made sense. And then a question occurred to him. "How did you manage to get up to that part of the ranch the day of the hurricane?"

She shrugged. "I drove as far as I could and then when the going got really rough, I went the rest of the way on foot." At the time, it hadn't seemed like such a big deal.

Jonah's brow furrowed as he thought over what she had just told him. He reviewed the scene in his mind when he'd gone out to search for her. "I didn't see a car when I got there."

Maggie frowned. "That's because it was probably swept away in the flash flood," she admitted ruefully. "I haven't seen it since that day." She turned her head toward him, the expression on her face daring him to lecture her.

Jonah thought it best to focus on the positive aspects. "Well, the threat of the flood is over and the waters have all been receding. If nothing unexpected happens, water levels should be back to normal within the week. Who knows?" he speculated. "Maybe your car'll turn up."

"Maybe," Maggie echoed, although she really wasn't holding out any hope that she was going to find it "washed up" somewhere. "But if it does show up, most likely it won't be in any condition to be driven." It would probably be far too waterlogged for that.

"And *that* is the reason why we're going to go there on horseback," he told her.

Which brought up more questions for her. "We're going to be riding out on Cody?" she asked, remembering her rescue and how Jonah had brought her to his cabin with the two of them riding on his horse.

"*I'm* riding Cody," he corrected. "You'll be on Strawberry." Before she could ask, he told her, "That's one of the extra mounts the team brought with us. We use Strawberry and the others interchangeably when our own horses need to be switched out."

"Strawberry?" Maggie repeated, the name giving her hope. "Is she gentle?"

"She has a good disposition," Jonah assured her, adding, "Don't worry, I wouldn't put you on the back of a bucking bronco even if you told me you were an accomplished rider."

That should have comforted her, Maggie thought, but it really didn't. She saw the stable just ahead and instantly felt a knot forming in her stomach.

Pulling up the hand brake as he parked his truck, Jonah leaned in toward Maggie and told her confidently, "Don't worry, you can do this."

Maggie had never liked being thought of as inept,

but she wasn't the type to make a show of false bravado, either.

"Right. Easy for you to say," she murmured, getting out.

"And easy for you to do," he assured her, sensing that what Maggie needed was to have someone display unwavering confidence in her. He joined her outside the truck. "Cody and I will be right beside you."

"Doing what?" Maggie asked. "Laughing?"

"I'm not planning on laughing," Jonah told her so seriously that she believed him.

"Okay," she answered haltingly as she followed Jonah into the stable. "I'll try hard not to give you anything to laugh at."

"Sounds like a plan," he replied good-naturedly. "Tell you what, in the interest of time, I'll skip teaching you the proper way to saddle a horse and just go ahead and saddle both horses for us—this time."

She didn't understand. That sounded rather ominous to her. "*This* time?" Maggie questioned.

"Yes," he replied simply, taking his saddle and placing it on Cody. Maggie all but shrank against the stall's walls. "The next time we go out, I'll expect you to follow my directions—unless you already know how to properly saddle a horse?" He left his question up in the air, waiting for her to address it one way or another.

Lying would only get her into trouble. Besides, she had found that she didn't like being on the receiving end of lies, so the idea of lying herself was rather off-putting to her.

Which meant that Maggie had no choice but to tell him the truth. "The few times I attempted to ride a horse, someone else saddled the horse for me."

Jonah nodded. "I thought as much," he said, but there was no note of superiority in his voice, no condescension, either. As far as he was concerned, Jonah was just telling her his assumptions on the matter.

Maggie moved to one side, allowing Jonah to have unobstructed access to the horse he'd told her she would be riding. This way, he could saddle the mare for her quickly.

Jonah's movements were smooth, she observed, almost as if he didn't even have to think about them. He just went ahead and did what needed to be done. He had probably been doing this all his life, Maggie mused.

Jonah saddled both horses in less time than it would have taken her to saddle just the one. But then, given what he did for a living, that only seemed natural.

Finished, Jonah held on to Strawberry's reins as he turned toward Maggie.

"Okay," he announced, "your horse is all ready to go."

Maggie wasn't aware of running the tip of her tongue along her very dry lips, but Jonah was. He could almost *feel* himself being drawn in as he watched her. Not only that, but he found himself fighting a very strong urge to sample those very same lips.

"That makes one of us," she murmured moving a little closer.

"C'mon," Jonah urged. "I'll give you a boost up," he offered. "Hold on to the reins." He handed them over to her. Their hands brushed and it occurred to him that her fingertips were absolutely icy. She was really nervous about doing this, he realized. "Put one foot into the stirrup and then swing the other leg over the back of the horse," he coached. "I'll be right here."

She followed instructions, almost freezing in mid-motion. She felt his hand lightly making contact with her posterior, just enough to get her to complete the mount without an incident—or falling.

"Getting on the horse isn't the problem," she told him once she was finally seated in the saddle. "*Staying* on the horse, however, might be."

He wanted to get moving, but not at the cost of having something happen to Maggie. She badly needed to build up her confidence.

"Then we'll take it slow," he promised her.

Watching Jonah swing effortlessly into his own saddle, Maggie couldn't help thinking that he was the very picture of ease as he sat astride Cody.

"Keep a light—but firm—hold on the reins and press your knees against Strawberry's thighs," he instructed. "Remember," he reminded her seriously, "you're the one in charge."

"In charge. Right," Maggie laughed dryly at the

idea. "I'm not sure that Strawberry's aware that she got that memo."

"Then *make* her aware of it. Don't worry," Jonah said as if he could read Maggie's thoughts. "Strawberry expects to be directed around."

Maggie sincerely had her doubts about that. "You sure about that?" she questioned. She wasn't the type to impose her will on others, that included horses.

"I'm sure," he answered. "But that doesn't mean that she's not going to try to test you." He thought of another way for her to approach the problem. "Think of Strawberry as if she was a kid. Kids expect to be told what to do, but that doesn't stop them from trying to test the boundary lines that have been drawn around them."

The analogy amused Maggie. He might actually have something there. "Like I said, you're going to make a good father someday."

Holding her breath, Maggie tested what he'd told her to do and pressed her knees against the mare's flanks. In response, the animal sped up a little.

"Hey, it worked," Maggie cried in surprise.

"Told you." Jonah grinned, pleased. "Just keep telling yourself that you're the one in charge. If you believe it," he stressed, "Strawberry will believe it."

Maggie still had her doubts about that, but she was a little more willing to give it a try—especially with Jonah riding beside her. She had absolutely no doubts that if something were to go wrong, he would jump in and rescue her. After all, it was in his nature. He had already done it once. Rescuing her from a runaway horse had to be a lot easier than finding and rescuing her from the ravages of a hurricane.

"You look more confident," Jonah observed several minutes later as they made their way toward the tree that Adam Corgan had singled out on the map he had sent along with his posthumous note.

"That's all your doing," Maggie responded. She wasn't about to accept any compliments that she felt she hadn't really earned.

"No, it's not," he countered. "I could talk myself blue in the face, telling you what to do and how to do it. But you're the one who took that advice and put it to use. So, the way I see it, the credit belongs strictly to you." He gave her a penetrating look. "So just accept it."

The smile that formed slowly on her lips made Maggie beam. The expression turned a beautiful woman into something even more. It made her into someone who could create an ache inside him.

Rousing himself, Jonah shifted his attention back to the reason why they were out here in the first place, searching for clues about someone who possibly didn't even exist.

"You think this is a fool's errand, don't you?" she asked him, her question breaking into his thoughts.

Jonah framed his reply cautiously. "I'd say it's too soon to tell."

"But if you had to make a guess?" Maggie pressed.

"Before I did that," he qualified, "I'd want the answer to other questions." He saw her raise an eyebrow.

"Like why now? Why send you on this scavenger hunt without even telling you what it is you're looking for? Why is the only thing that the dearly departed *did* specify is that whatever you find—*if* you find it—will provide a 'truth' that will make his brother, a convicted six-time serial killer, 'free'?" he asked. The missive in the note didn't make any sense to him. "Is 'free' just meant in the poetic sense, or is there actually something there that would tell us that Elliott Corgan is really not guilty of all those murders? *Those* are the questions I want the answers to," he told her.

Maggie sighed, trying not to allow a wave of hopelessness to slip in. "Those are a lot of questions," she finally agreed.

Maybe he shouldn't have laid it out like that, Jonah thought. But now that he had, he asked Maggie, "Got any answers?"

She shook her head. "I don't even have one."

He had another, possibly easier question for her to answer.

"When you were up that tree, did you happen to see anything from that vantage point?" he asked. There was a possibility that perhaps Maggie saw something that she didn't even realize she was seeing.

"The only thing I saw were rising waters," she answered.

Until Jonah had come riding up like a real live hero, she had started to seriously worry that maybe she *wasn't* going to make it back for her sister's wedding. The thought of the water rising so high that it would eventually engulf her had become an increasingly serious concern for her.

"But you didn't see anything else?" he asked.

"To be honest," she admitted, "nothing else was on my mind except getting back to town for my sister's wedding. When I saw you riding up on Cody like some white knight out of a story about King Arthur and his Round Table, my heart stopped. I could have sworn you had a gleaming white light shining all around you like some huge halo."

He grinned at her narrative. "That would be my saving-a-damsel-in-distress aura," Jonah told her—and then laughed. "I'm just really glad I was able to find you."

"That makes two of us," she told him in all honesty. The next moment, she realized that they had ridden up to the tree in question.

Cody was trained to remain where he was once Jonah dropped his reins and they touched the ground. Swinging off the horse now, he turned toward Maggie. "I'll help you down," he offered.

If she had any confidence in her abilities to sit astride a horse, she might have told him that she was perfectly capable of getting down herself. But she hadn't built up that sort of confidence. Luckily, her common sense wasn't in short supply.

Meeting his offer to help with a simple, "Thank you," she gratefully allowed him to put his hands on her waist in order to help her dismount. She was itching to begin the search.

# Chapter 9

Taking hold of her waist, Jonah eased Maggie off her horse. She slid down, her body not even a whisper away from his.

By the time her feet touched the ground, all sorts of alarms had begun going off in every inch of her throbbing body.

And by the expression on Jonah's ruggedly handsome face, she could tell that she wasn't the only one whose body temperature had risen from a normal 98.6 degrees to a temperature that was just too high to be measured by a regular thermometer.

Maggie was even more unclear about what happened next. For the life of her, she wasn't sure exactly *who* made the first move.

Maybe it was simultaneous, born and executed in the heat of the moment.

She didn't know—she didn't care. All she was aware of was the intense yearning that washed over her. She was aware of that and of the overwhelming kiss that all but exploded between them.

He kissed her.

She kissed him.

They kissed each other.

Exactly who instigated that first kiss was utterly moot—except for the all-consuming effect that occurred in the wake of lips meeting lips.

Maggie gave in to the feeling instantly, as if she had been waiting all of her life for this one moment, this one occurrence.

Maybe, looking back, she had been. James had *never* kissed her like this.

Rising up on her toes, Maggie immediately lost herself in this kiss. She was aware of everything going on within the small, tight sphere that only the two of them occupied. The rest of the world wasn't there. All that mattered was that he was.

Jonah hadn't meant for this to happen, although he would have called himself a liar if he hadn't admitted to thinking about this.

Longing for this.

Ever since he had arrived back in Whisperwood and saw Maggie from across the room, talking to his brother Donovan and her sister, desire had slowly taken root within him. Once rooted, it continued to flower and spread with a vengeance despite his efforts to keep it all under control.

But the moment her body had made contact with his, it was as if a blazing lightning bolt had flashed through him, disarming him even as it temporarily disengaged his common sense.

Jonah cupped the back of her head as his lips came down on hers, claiming her. Branding her.

Branding him.

He felt far more alive than he had in years.

His heart was pounding so fast, sending adrenaline racing throughout his entire body, as if there was a need to alert every single fiber of his being that there was something magnificent going on.

Something to celebrate.

Jonah slanted his mouth over Maggie's again and again, the kiss growing deeper and more consuming each time until they were both utterly submerged in it.

Maggie could feel him wanting her. They were out here, all alone in the world except for the horses. There was no one to see them.

The conditions were far from ideal, but right now, she didn't care.

She—

Moving backward to get a better footing, Maggie felt her heel hitting something and she stumbled. Startled, she gasped, her lips breaking away from Jonah's.

His arms quickly closed around her. If they hadn't, she would have fallen backward and wound up on the ground.

"Maggie?" Surprise underscored her name, and Jonah looked at her, confused.

With the moment abruptly stolen from them, Maggie looked down to see what she had stumbled on. She thought she saw something white-ish poking up out of the ground. Her brow furrowed as she tried to look closer.

What *was* that?

She was certain that the last time she had been at this location, that white thing had *not* been here, or at least not sticking out. The floods and winds had played havoc with the dirt and leaves that had been clustered at the foot of the tree, gathering at that spot since forever. The hurricane was responsible for clearing it all away and exposing whatever that was underneath.

At a loss as to what was going on, Jonah continued holding on to her. He searched her face. "Are you okay?" he asked.

"I will be once—"

She didn't get to finish her sentence and maybe that was just as well because she had almost said something about her racing heart. Instead, she looked down again, staring at what she'd thought was a white stick.

That was when she realized that it wasn't a stick at all.

A scream rose in her throat, but she managed to stifle it. However, her eyes, flying open so wide they made him think of proverbial saucers, gave her away.

Grabbing his arm, she pointed to what was protruding out of the earth. In a hushed whisper, she asked, "What *is* that, Jonah?"

For the first time, he looked down at the ground. What she was pointing out didn't make any sense to him. Jonah dropped to his knees beside the newly uncovered article to get a closer, better look at it.

Gathering her courage, Maggie knelt down beside him.

"Omigod, is that—" She had to swallow in order to produce enough saliva to allow her to say the word and not have it stick inside her mouth. "Is that a bone?"

Taking his handkerchief out, Jonah cleared away the remaining dirt that was clinging to it. "It's a bone all right."

"Is it human?" she whispered.

"It certainly could be." Before he could say anything further, he saw that Maggie had started digging in the dirt that was just beneath where they had found the bone. He caught her hand, momentarily stilling it. "Maggie, maybe you should wait for the police chief."

But she shook her head, rejecting that idea. "This might not be what we think it is and then we've gotten him out here for nothing. He's got enough to deal with with the flood and everything else. We need to be sure this is an actual human body before we drag him out here."

"You're right," he agreed. "But only dig just enough so that we can be sure it *is* a human body. The second we are, we'll stop digging." It wasn't a suggestion.

"Stop talking and start digging," she insisted, sinking her hands into the muck and moving as much as she could each time.

* * *

It didn't take long for them to find the rest of it. The rest of the body. The bone that Maggie had accidentally stumbled across had somehow been separated from the rest of the skeleton. That was the result of either some scavenging animal searching for food, or maybe even the hurricane itself.

When they had cleared away the dirt and debris, Maggie stared in horror at what had been uncovered. It was the fully mummified skeletal remains of what appeared to be a woman, due to the larger, rounded pelvis region.

And then it suddenly dawned on her. "This is it," Maggie cried, looking up at Jonah. "This is what Adam Corgan wanted me to find."

It didn't make any sense to him. "How is finding this woman supposed to set Elliott Corgan free?" Jonah questioned. He looked back at the skeleton. "And who is she?"

Maggie struggled not to think of the skeleton as the remains of what had once been a living, breathing human being, but just as the embodiment of a puzzle. She looked down at the mummified body. There were no clues, no indication who she had once been. Nothing to identify the woman.

"I have no idea who that is," she confessed.

"Well, maybe the chief might be able to tell us," Jonah speculated. "Thompson's been part of this town it seems like forever. According to my parents, he was definitely on the police force when all this went down." Getting up, he offered his hand to Maggie and helped her to her feet. "He must have heard about a missing girl, one who hadn't been accounted for when those other bodies—seven in all—started turning up in shallow graves."

She still seemed a little uncertain about bringing this to the chief's attention. "He told us not to get involved," she reminded Jonah.

"Well, we obviously are," he said, gesturing toward the preserved remains. "And he's got more important things on his mind than to take us to task for not listening to his advice." Jonah looked back at the body. "For one thing, he's now got an unidentified mummified body to deal with."

"So are we going to ride back into town to tell him?" she asked Jonah.

He didn't think that was a good idea. "I don't think we should leave the body. You never know, another animal might make off with part of it. Besides, we don't even know if the chief is in town. He might be anywhere." Jonah took out his cell phone from his back pocket and held it up. "I've got a signal! The lines have finally been restored," he told her. He looked at his phone to double-check. There were bars. "We'll call Thompson and tell him what we've found."

Maggie looked down at the mummified body again. "He's going to be thrilled," she murmured.

"Thrilled or not," Jonah said, "the chief needs to be told."

The cell phone on the other end of the number that Jonah had keyed in rang a total of nine times. On the tenth ring, he knew his call was about to go to voice mail. Just then a gruff voice picked up and answered, warning him, "This had better be an emergency and it had better be good."

Jonah looked down at the mummified remains wrapped in plastic. "Well, it definitely qualifies as an emergency. As for the other part, it all depends on your definition of 'good.'"

"Is that you, Jonah?" Chief Thompson questioned, although he was fairly certain that it was.

In his haste to get the chief down here, Jonah realized that he hadn't identified himself. The lines might be up, but obviously caller ID wasn't functioning yet.

"Yes, it is," Jonah said.

A trace of annoyance came through. "Jonah, what the hell are you going on about?"

"Well, Chief, I'm out here with Maggie Reeves," Jonah began.

"Where's 'here'?" the chief asked.

"Live Oak Ranch," Jonah said quickly. He didn't wait for the chief to say anything further but dived straight into the heart of the reason he was calling. "And we're looking at what appears to be the mummified remains of possibly a young woman. There's nothing near the body to tell us who she is."

There was a long pause on the other end and Jonah thought he might have lost the connection. But then the chief's booming voice came on, calling him on the carpet. "I thought I told you two to stay clear of all this."

"You did say that, Chief," Jonah agreed, steering

the conversation in another direction. "And we really weren't looking for them. Maggie and I just happened to find the remains totally by accident," Jonah said, his eyes slanting toward Maggie. He wanted to protect her from the chief's anger.

"Uh-huh." Anyone could tell that the chief didn't believe him, Jonah thought. "Just where are you on the ranch?"

"We're right on the site of the ranch's biggest oak tree, the one the Corgans claimed is the oldest tree in the whole state. Are you familiar with it?" Jonah asked Thompson.

"I'm familiar with it," the chief replied. His voice was strangely devoid of all emotion and sounded as if he was half-dead inside.

"Well, we found the body right near the tree," Jonah told him. "I guess the hurricane must have blown away all the dirt that killer used to bury the body in his attempt to hide it from anyone's view," he added, trying to get some sort of a response from the chief.

Thompson sighed. "All right, since you found this body, I want you to stay right there with it," the chief instructed. "I'm coming out with my forensic team to see if the killer left any evidence."

"I don't think they're going to have much luck, not after the hurricane went barreling through here," Jonah told him.

"We'll see," the chief said, his tone still unreadable.

Sensing that the chief was about to hang up, Jonah

had one last thing to ask him. "Hey, Chief, do you have any idea who this last girl might have been?"

"Yeah," Thompson answered grimly. "I do have an idea."

When the chief didn't say anything beyond that, Jonah pressed the man, "Well? Who was it?"

Jonah thought he heard the chief make some sort of noise, but he wasn't certain. "I'll talk to you when I get there," Thompson said almost curtly just before he terminated the call.

"What did he say?" Maggie asked the second Jonah put his phone away. "The chief's got a booming voice, but I couldn't make out everything. He's coming, right?"

"Yes, he's coming," Jonah told her. "And he's bringing his forensic team with him."

Maggie nodded, pleased. "Well, that's good." She thought of the last thing that she'd heard Jonah say to the chief. "Did he say he knew who this was, or that he at least suspected who it might be?"

Jonah shook his head. "No, he cut me off when I asked."

Maggie frowned. "That's not like Chief Thompson," Maggie noted. "If anything, he's usually very outgoing and friendly."

Jonah shrugged. "Well, I guess this hurricane has been hard on everyone," he told her. "It's been making people behave in ways that they didn't think they ever would."

She looked at him. Was Jonah talking about the chief, or was he possibly referring to himself? Specifically, was he referring to what had happened between them seconds before she'd accidentally uncovered that mummified skeleton?

Maggie felt her cheeks growing warm. If she hadn't taken that step back and tripped on it, who knew what might have happened?

She had felt him responding to her. It wasn't all in her head. He'd wanted her as much as she had wanted him. Both of them had been lost in the heat of the moment and they could have easily taken it to the next level and gone further.

The idea of making love right on top of a hidden skeleton was appalling to her now that she knew the body had been there, but at the time, they hadn't known anything except the hunger that was so obviously consuming both of them.

She shivered, thinking how grateful she was that fate had intervened when it did. What if they had gone along with their erupting passions, if they had made love right then and there? Once they discovered that they had come together right on top of the wrapped-up remains of a murder victim—because it was obvious that was what she must be—what might have been the beginning of something beautiful would have been forever tainted. They would never be able to look at one another without remembering that they had made love on top of a murdered woman's hidden grave.

Jonah watched Maggie's expression change. She was obviously thinking about the dead woman again. And judging by her face, Maggie's thoughts were unsettling.

"Are you okay?" he asked her gently, still watching her for any indication that she wasn't telling him everything.

"You mean other than feeling sick to my stomach because we just found the remains of a mummified murder victim?" Maggie asked.

"You're right." He understood what Maggie was implying. "That was a stupid question I just asked. As soon as the chief gets here with his team, I'll take you home."

"The hell you will," she said with such effusive spirit that it surprised him. "I'm not going anywhere. I want to find out who she is."

Jonah sighed. He shouldn't have been surprised. The Maggie Reeves he had come to know these last few days wasn't about to retreat and go home if her questions weren't answered.

## Chapter 10

They didn't have that long to wait, which was good, because every extra moment she had to occupy in the same vicinity as the wrapped-up, mummified skeleton was beyond unsettling for Maggie. Her heart leaped when she heard the sound of the chief's all-terrain vehicle coming closer and approaching the area where they were.

It had taken less than an hour for the chief to come, but it felt a great deal longer than that.

The chief's vehicle was followed by the van containing three members of the crime scene investigative team.

Jonah caught a glimpse of Maggie's face. It didn't take a genius to guess what was behind the look she was wearing.

"They would have made better time getting here if they had come on horseback," he told her, knowing that Maggie had to have felt that the chief and his team using vehicles to get here supported her own desire to do the same.

"I guess we'll never find out," she replied tersely. "The point is, they're finally here."

The next moment, there was no longer time for any sort of a debate on the subject. The chief had gotten out of his Jeep and was heading straight for them. The man looked as if he was loaded for bear. She really wasn't in any sort of a mood for a lecture.

Looking at the chief, she could have sworn that she almost saw steam coming out of Thompson's ears. The scowl on the man's face would have stopped a hardened criminal in his tracks.

"I thought I told you two to keep clear of this investigation." Thompson all but growled the words at the duo. The chief was as close to being furious as Maggie had ever seen the man. He appeared weary, but his eyes were flashing. "You need to leave this kind of thing to the professionals. Colton, you of all people should understand that. I would have expected this kind of Nancy Drew behavior from Maggie here, but you, you really should have known better," he told Jonah, vainly trying to keep his voice down.

Maggie didn't feel right about having someone else take the blame for something that she had instigated. She remained silent for as long as she could, but inevitably, she lost the fight.

Surprising both the chief and Jonah, she stepped in between the two men.

"Don't go yelling at Jonah, Chief," she warned sharply. "It wasn't his fault. I was the one who wanted to come out here again and take a second look around. Jonah just came with me to make sure that I was safe and didn't get into any trouble."

"Maggie," Jonah began, trying to pull her aside before she got carried away.

But Maggie had gotten all wound up. She had no intention of standing by meekly as Thompson gave Jonah a dressing-down for something that she was responsible for getting underway.

Putting her hand up to indicate that she hadn't finished talking yet, Maggie informed the chief, "And it's a lucky thing that I did, because if we *hadn't* come back up here, then who knows *when* this body would have been found?" she asked. "The poor thing might have gone another thirty, forty years before she was finally discovered."

Thompson appeared to be doing a slow boil. "Are you finished?" he asked in his deep, authoritative voice.

Maggie felt a little intimidated, but did her damnedest not to show it.

"Yes, I am. For now," she added as an afterthought in case anything else occurred to her in the next few minutes.

Both she and Jonah expected the chief to explode, but instead, all he did was nod curtly. "All right then, the forensic team will get on with its work and you two are free to go." Thompson waved toward the path he assumed they had taken to get here. "As a matter of fact, I think you should," he snapped.

Thompson turned away from them and returned to the body that had been carefully lifted from its grave, a grave that appeared to have been dug far deeper than the graves of the other women who had been killed.

Maggie regretted having become so combative with Thompson. There was something about the set of his shoulders that suggested to her a man in pain. The image tugged at her heart. She knew that his body language had nothing to do with the fact that she'd yelled at him. But there was something else going on here. Something that was deeply affecting the chief.

"Maggie, let's go," Jonah urged as he reached for her arm.

But Maggie drew her arm away before he could take hold of it. Instead, she moved a little closer to the chief, peering at his face.

"You know who that is, don't you, Chief?" she asked quietly.

"Yes, I do." The chief's voice was solemn, heavy. He didn't look at Maggie. Instead, he continued staring at the mummified remains lying on the ground not too far away. Maggie thought she saw tears gathering in the chief's eyes. "I wasn't sure until just now, but yes, I know who that is."

He picked up his head and looked at the two people who had discovered the body. "That's my little sister, Emmeline." His voice tightened as he told them, "See that bracelet on her left wrist?"

Maggie had noticed the bracelet when she and Jonah had cleared debris away from the body. Small, thin and delicate, the bracelet had what looked like tiny roses embossed along the length of it.

"Yes," she answered, waiting for the chief to continue.

"I gave that to Emmeline for her birthday." He laughed shortly at the memory. "She was always losing things. She lost the bracelet the very first week after I gave it to her." He pressed his lips together to regain control over his voice. "She had all her friends looking for it. She was so relieved when it finally turned up." He blew out a breath, the memory weighing heavily on his chest. "Emmeline was afraid of losing it again so she had the two ends welded together so that it couldn't come loose again. That way, she said, she'd always have it and it would remind her of me."

Thompson took in another long breath, as if that somehow helped to clear his mind. "I always knew that Elliott Corgan must have killed her, although he denied it when I questioned him." The chief's jaw hardened as he all but spit the words out. "Corgan said he wasn't the kind of man who would take credit for another man's work."

"Maybe he didn't do it," Jonah ventured, thinking that maybe the killer had been honest for once in his life.

Thompson gave him an incredulous look. "Why

would you say something like that?" he demanded. "This is Corgan land. Elliott's younger brother all but drew Maggie a map where she could find Emmeline's grave. We've got Elliott serving life in prison for killing six other women. It's not exactly a giant leap from there to the conclusion that he killed my sister."

Jonah wasn't completely convinced, although it pained him to argue with the chief, a man he both respected and liked. "But didn't you say that all the other women were buried in shallow graves?" he asked Thompson.

"Yes," the chief answered impatiently. "It's a matter of record."

"But your sister's grave was dug much deeper and her body was painstakingly well preserved," Maggie pointed out, picking up the thread of Jonah's argument. "If the same man who killed all those other women killed your sister, why go through all that extra trouble? Why did he single this particular victim out and give her this special treatment?"

Thompson lost his temper. "How the hell am I supposed to know what went on in that degenerate's head?" the chief demanded. "There could have been all sorts of reasons why he did things differently when it came to—" his voice faltered before he pushed on "—Emma's murder. The man's a deranged, insane serial killer."

Thompson threw up his hands. "Maybe he just wanted to mix things up. Or maybe he wanted us to waste our time, talking this to death and taking it apart while he has himself a good laugh over it.

I don't know," the chief stressed angrily, shouting at them. And then, realizing that he had crossed a line, Thompson took a moment to compose himself. "Look, I want you two to leave this alone. Do I make myself clear?" the chief demanded, looking from one to the other.

"Perfectly," Maggie replied a bit guardedly.

Her heart went out to the man, but at the same time, she felt that he was making a mistake, barring them from looking into this. For one thing, it was clear that her late father-in-law obviously wanted her to get to the bottom of all this. Why, of course, was a completely different matter.

"Yes, sir," Jonah was saying. He took hold of Maggie's arm with the intent of leading her back to where their horses were waiting. "Loud and clear," he told the other man.

"Uh-huh," Thompson replied. It was clear by his tone that he was far from convinced that the two of them would take his words to heart this time.

Disappointed by the turn of events, Maggie wasn't aware that they had to return to town via horseback until she was practically standing right next to her mount. She was far from happy.

"We're going to be riding back?" she questioned.

"That's usually how it works," Jonah told her, amused. "We ride out on horseback. We have to return on horseback. It's either that, or we have to walk beside the horses. Take your pick," he teased.

Maggie didn't seem happy. "I'll ride. But I have

a feeling I'm going to be really sore by tomorrow morning."

"Only one way around that," he told her.

Was he going to share some magical rubbing ointment with her?

"Oh?" Maggie said, waiting for him to tell her about some secret cure he'd discovered.

"Just keep riding until it becomes second nature to you," he said. "You'll stop hurting then. Practice makes perfect."

She should have known he'd say something like that, Maggie thought. "Thanks, but if you don't mind, I'll just keep on using my car to get around."

Maggie stood beside her horse, not relishing the idea of getting back into the saddle. She was feeling rather drained by their discovery.

About to swing into his own saddle, Jonah stopped when he noticed the pensive expression on Maggie's face. "Want a boost?" he guessed.

What she wanted was to be driven back, but the chief and his team were all busy and would be for a couple of hours to come.

"Sure, why not?" she said.

The words were no sooner out of her mouth than Jonah was right there at her back, boosting her up into her saddle. She swallowed her surprised gasp as she felt Jonah's hands quickly guiding her up.

"All ready to go?" he asked her, swinging up into his own saddle.

Maggie turned back for one last look. The forensic team was scattered, spread out on several sides of the tree and adjacent ground. They were sketching, taking pictures and in general documenting the entire scene where the chief's sister had been found.

She sighed, turning back again. "Well, since the chief obviously doesn't want us around, sure, let's go."

"You know," Maggie said, once they had gotten clear of the chief and his men and were riding toward Whisperwood, "I used to think of Chief Thompson as a nice, friendly man. Now he's acting as if we were a pair of bungling, annoying civilians who were trying to mess up his crime scene."

"You've got to see that this is personal for Thompson," Jonah told her.

"That's why he should welcome all the help he can get," she insisted.

But Jonah looked at it from the chief's point of view. "He doesn't see it as help. He sees it as interfering."

Maggie grew annoyed. Jonah should be taking her side in this, not the chief's.

"That's because he's being closed-minded," she insisted. She thought of how they had gotten here in the first place. "Besides, I have a unique perspective on this."

"What you have," Jonah told her calmly, "is a note from a dead man who might have had his own reasons for taunting the chief." He glanced at her, not wanting to set her off, but trying to make her see this logically. "By your own admission, you and Adam Corgan never had a close relationship."

"We didn't have much of one at all," Maggie corrected.

"Aha, that's my point exactly," he told her. He warmed to his subject. "Why reach out from beyond the grave? Why get you involved in this at all?" he asked, examining the details. "You broke your ties to the family when you divorced Adam's son. Adam had no reason to pull you back in."

"Which are all very good questions," Maggie responded. "And I want to find the answers to all of them." She began talking faster, trying to get him to agree. "My gut instincts tell me that the answers to all those questions can be found if we just continue to conduct our own investigation into this mystery. And since the chief doesn't want us doing that, we need to be doing this on our own—as a team."

That caught him off guard. How did they get from just riding out to the old ranch to here? "When did we become a team?" he asked her.

She looked at him in surprise. "You don't want to be a team?" Maggie asked.

"I didn't say that," he told her. She was putting words into his mouth, he thought. "I was just curious when this momentous pairing occurred."

She thought that was obvious. "I guess that happened the first time you took me along to help you conduct a search and rescue effort."

He supposed he could see her point. He wasn't about to argue with it, that was for sure. "If I had known that, I might have marked the occasion with a little speech," he told her.

Her mouth quirked a little in a grin. "I guess we all dodged a bullet there."

"So we're partners?" he asked, wanting to be sure exactly where they stood in this.

She nodded. "Partners. At least when it comes to this," she qualified. Thinking back to the kiss they'd shared, she felt it necessary to add, "Just don't get any funny ideas."

"Well, these are very serious times, thanks to the hurricane—and the murders," he replied. "I'd say that we have to take our laughter where we find it," he told her significantly.

Maggie shifted on her horse. She wasn't comfortable, not on horseback or with the subject matter. Both made her feel vulnerable.

"So, where to now?" she asked when she realized that she wasn't sure if they really *were* headed for town or some other destination.

"Still a lot of search and rescue work to be done, not to mention that there's still a lot of debris to be cleared away." Jonah realized that he was just taking for granted that she was up for this. "Look, if you're tired, or just want to recharge, I can drop you off at the cabin and take the horse back to the stable. Your call."

That was the last thing she wanted. "If it's all the same to you, I'd rather not be alone with my thoughts right now."

There was sympathy in his voice when he asked, "Finding that mummified body really got to you, didn't it?"

She laughed dryly and nodded. "I could have lived my whole life without seeing that."

That hadn't been his idea. "You're the one who wanted to go there and look around," he reminded her.

"I know, I know," she was quick to acknowledge. "I can't help it if I'm curious. It's a congenital defect," she told him.

She said it with such a straight face, he wondered if she actually believed what she was saying was true.

"Maybe I'm here to save you from yourself," Jonah said.

"And maybe I'm here to get you to use your special skill set of finding things to see if we can find just what Adam meant by that message he left and, more importantly, that you use those skills to help find out if the chief's sister was really killed by the same serial killer who's currently behind bars."

"We'll see," was all that Jonah was willing to say on the subject for now.

He felt it was safer that way.

# *Chapter 11*

As far as hurricanes went, the lifespan of this particular one had been mercifully short. However the short amount of time did not minimize the damage that Hurricane Brooke did both physically and emotionally to the people of Whisperwood who had found themselves on the receiving end of the hurricane's sweeping effects. Added to that were the people who had not suffered losses, losing neither their homes nor any of the people they loved, but were still affected. Those were the people who were suffering from the acute effects of survivor guilt. Those were the people who were haunted by one question. Why were they spared when those around them were not?

Jonah found himself at a loss when he tried to

comfort one of these guilt-ridden survivors to absolutely no avail.

Maggie felt sorry for both Jonah and the woman he'd been vainly trying to comfort. With her heart going out to Jonah, she quietly inserted herself into the scene, much to his obvious surprise and relief.

Taking his place, Maggie looked at the woman who had broken down in uncontrollable sobs when Jonah had asked her how she was doing.

Instead of shrinking back from Kayla, a young woman who she knew by sight but had never gotten close to beyond that, Maggie tried to put herself in the thirty-four-year-old woman's place.

Mentally she asked herself how *she* would react in a situation like this. It gave her a great deal of empathy for the anguish that Kayla was suffering.

"Why?" Kayla asked her, her voice cracking. "Why am I still here and not Jacob? He was the better person, not me."

"Instead of trying to find the response to something that you have no real way of ever knowing the answer to, why don't you make up your mind that you are going to be the best version of yourself that you can possibly be?" Maggie gently told the woman.

Kayla's sobs slowly subsided. She raised her red-rimmed eyes and looked into Maggie's. She struggled a couple of minutes, attempting to catch her breath. "I don't under—understand," she cried.

"Try to help the people around you. Comfort them, offer to listen. Right now, people are more vulnerable than they have *ever* been in their lives. They need to feel that they can make it through this, that there *is* a light at the end of the tunnel even if they can't see it yet. Help them to think positive. You'll wind up helping them as well as yourself," Maggie told the other woman. "That is why you were spared."

Kayla was still fighting back her sobs. "You really think so?"

Maggie never hesitated. "I really think so," she said, squeezing the shaking hands that had been clutching hers.

"All right, I'll try," the other woman said. There was still a hitch in her voice.

"That's all anyone can ever ask," Maggie said, giving Kayla a long, warm embrace. The other woman seemed to take heart from that.

"That was pretty good," Jonah said to Maggie several minutes later when they finally walked away, leaving Kayla with one of the other survivors. "How did you come up with that on the spur of the moment?" he couldn't help asking.

"Easy," she answered. "I just put myself in her place and told her what I would have wanted someone to tell me." And then she elaborated. "That I was important in the scheme of things. That I didn't survive by accident but for a reason—so I could help others come to grips with their own losses. What?" Maggie asked when she saw the way that Jonah was looking at her.

"Nothing. I was just thinking how amazing you are—and how glad I am that I was able to find you before you wound up falling out of that tree and hurting yourself," he added.

She had no idea what possessed her to ask Jonah the next question, but before she could censor herself, the question just came tumbling out. "Is that the only reason you're glad you found me?"

Jonah turned his head toward her, and the way he looked at her sent a shiver running up and down her spine.

"I think you already know the answer to that," Jonah told her, his voice low, caressing.

The desire to kiss her was almost overpowering. But they were out where everyone could see them, and he didn't want anyone gossiping about Maggie. Besides, once things were back to normal and his brother was married, he would be on his way back to Austin. He didn't want to leave Maggie to deal with unwanted speculation on her own. It wouldn't be right.

"Why don't I drop you off at the cabin—" he began, only to have her cut in.

"Drop me off?" she repeated, confused. "Why? Where will you be?" she asked. Earlier he'd made it sound as if they would be working together for the rest of the day.

He hadn't even wanted to say this to Maggie. Jonah knew that the mere mention of her apartment would sadden her. But he wasn't about to lie to her, either.

"I'm just going to see how cleanup is going around the Towers. You've done enough for one day—more than enough," he emphasized, thinking of the body that had been uncovered. "Why don't you take it easy and I'll come to the cabin in a little while?"

She didn't like the idea of resting—or being alone with her thoughts. "I can help," Maggie insisted as she followed him to his truck.

"I know you can," he told her. "But you don't have to feel like you need to keep proving yourself to anyone over and over again. Trust me, I get it," he assured Maggie. "Now get some rest before you wear yourself completely out." He thought it might help if he filled her in about what was going on. "We've got a bulldozer coming in to clear away the larger debris so we can get started rebuilding that area. It looks like the Towers sustained the most amount of damage."

An ironic smile played on Maggie's lips. "It figures."

He could almost *see* what thoughts were going on in her head. "Take your own advice, Maggie, and stop overthinking things."

"You sure you don't want me there?" she asked as he drove them to his cabin.

"I'm sure," Jonah said firmly.

Maggie shrugged, sinking back in the passenger seat and surrendering. "I guess you're right. Besides, the chances of my finding anything in that pile of rubble are pretty nonexistent anyway."

The wistful note in her voice caught his attention and Jonah looked at her. "Completely," he agreed, even though it pained him to do so. "Why, what is it that you'd try to look for?"

She felt almost silly talking about this, but she had been the one who had started this, so she answered his question. "I had this snow globe as a kid. My dad gave it to me for my birthday. I don't remember which one," she said honestly. "I was five, or maybe six. Anyway, the globe had a puppy in the center of a snowstorm—at least it was a snowstorm when I shook the globe," she amended. "I must have spent hours when I was a kid, just watching the snow coming down and engulfing that dog."

Realizing what she had to sound like, Maggie laughed at herself. "I guess I was easily entertained, but it's the one thing I remember my dad giving me. He wasn't very big on gifts," she confided.

"I can look for it," Jonah told her. "But to be honest—"

She nodded. "I know there's no way it could have survived that hurricane. At the very least, the globe probably shattered when the apartment came down," she said, ending his sentence for him.

He was pulling up in front of his cabin.

"Are you going to be okay here?" Jonah asked as she began to get out. He suddenly felt as if he was abandoning a waif, leaving her alone in the cabin.

She smiled at his concern. Jonah was a good man, she thought. He'd proven it over and over again.

Maggie tried to set his mind at ease. "As long as there's not another hurricane on its way, I'll be fine."

Still, he didn't like leaving her alone. But he liked dragging her over to the ruins of the Towers even less. He chose the lesser of the two evils.

"I'll be back as soon as I check in to see how everything's going," Jonah promised.

"Take your time," Maggie told him, one hand on the doorknob as she opened the cabin door. "You don't have to rush on my account."

But he did, Jonah thought as he pulled away from the cabin, watching Maggie grow smaller in his rearview mirror. He did have to rush on her account because he wanted to get back to her as soon as he possibly could. Despite her swaggering displays of independence, there was something about Maggie Reeves that brought out his protective nature.

She might come on like gangbusters, the way she had around the chief this morning, but she didn't fool him. He saw the vulnerable woman under all that and he had this overwhelming desire to keep her safe even though the immediate danger, according to the weather reports, had passed.

But he had been at this job long enough to know that there were all sorts of dangers to be afraid of, not just the ones that could be heard about on weather forecasts.

Maybe *he* was the one who was letting his imagination get carried away, Jonah told himself.

He pressed down harder on the gas pedal.

The second she closed the door behind her, she felt it. The cabin seemed eerily silent to her without Jonah there. She wasn't the sort of person who was afraid of the dark or who held her breath, waiting to hear something go "bump" in the night. Still, Maggie decided that having a light on while she made dinner out of whatever she could find in the refrigerator wasn't all that bad an idea, even though it wasn't dark outside yet.

If one light was good, several lights were even better, she decided, switching on the lamps and overhead lights in the kitchenette. For good measure, she put on the lights in the living room, as well.

Opening the refrigerator, she searched the crisper drawer and found that she had missed a quartered chicken the last time. She decided that she would use it to make fried chicken. It was simple, difficult to mess up and more importantly, she'd never met anyone who didn't like fried chicken.

Once she saw that Jonah had a little bit of flour and some oil in his pantry, she felt as if she had gotten a go-ahead sign and got started.

Maggie really had no idea if Jonah was going to be back soon the way he had promised, or if he would get caught up in something and be home a great deal later. Either way, she knew that fried chicken tasted good served hot or cold.

Maggie got started, taking her time with each step while humming fragments of a song under her breath. It was a familiar tune and the sound of it comforted her, although for the life of her, she couldn't remember more than five words from the lyrics.

Doing something as normal as making fried chicken helped to soothe her, as well.

She had just immersed the last piece of chicken in the flour mixture she'd created when she heard her cell phone begin to make a pulsing sound, demanding her attention. She paused to wipe her fingertips on a kitchen towel that had seen better days, then she pulled the phone out of her hip pocket. Maggie swiped across the screen even as her brain registered the fact that she didn't recognize the caller ID.

But then, maybe Jonah's phone had died and he had had to borrow someone else's phone to call her. Most likely he was calling to tell her that he was going to be late getting back. It was to be expected. Jonah felt he was indispensable and for the most part she had to admit that the man was right. Everyone turned to him for guidance.

Maggie caught herself smiling. If he was calling about that, then Jonah was also incredibly thoughtful.

But when she unlocked her phone, she saw that she wasn't getting an incoming call. Instead, it was a text message.

And the message wasn't from Jonah. It was coming from a blocked number.

Stop sticking your nose where it doesn't belong or you might not live to see another dawn.

Maggie stared at the screen, rereading the message. There was no mistaking the meaning of the text. It was definitely intended as a threat. But who would want to threaten her? And exactly *what* was this person referring to? What did he mean by "sticking her nose into" something? Was he talking about her finding that body on the Corgan ranch?

And *how* would this anonymous person even know anything about that? She and Jonah had only notified the chief this afternoon. Thompson had brought his forensic team with him when he arrived on the scene, but they were all part of the police department.

Was whoever had texted her this threat part of the police department, as well? Or had he hacked into the police department so he could keep tabs on what was going on?

Why would he want to?

Unless...

"Unless he's the killer," Maggie cried out loud.

"Unless who's the killer?" Jonah asked, picking that exact moment to walk into his cabin.

Maggie yelped and jumped. She'd been so caught up in trying to figure out who had sent her the threatening text, she hadn't heard Jonah pulling up in his truck.

*Great work, Maggie*, she berated herself. *Whoever wrote this text could have pulled up in a train and you wouldn't have heard him until he killed you.*

"And why do you have all the lights on?" Jonah asked just before he saw that the chicken pieces in the large frying pan were about to begin burning and smoking. Moving swiftly, he turned down the flame and pushed the pan onto another burner until it could cool off.

"Hey, is everything all right?" he questioned, crossing over to Maggie.

For the first time since he'd walked in, Jonah saw the frightened, distressed look on Maggie's face and the way she was clutching her phone.

"What happened here?" Jonah asked.

"Everything is fine," Maggie answered, her voice hardly louder than a squeak. There wasn't a shred of conviction in it.

"No, it's not," Jonah contradicted forcefully. He took hold of her shoulders and looked into her eyes. "Now tell me what's wrong."

Rather than say anything, she touched her screen to refresh the message, then handed her phone over to Jonah.

His expression hardened as he quickly scanned the message.

"Who sent you this?" he asked.

"I have no idea," she answered. "It came in as anonymous."

Maggie double-checked to make sure she hadn't missed anything that might indicate who the sender was. She hadn't.

Jonah didn't like this, but he didn't want to say anything that might fuel her fears further. "It's probably just a crank call from some pathetic idiot who gets off thinking he's frightening people with vague threats." His eyes narrowed as he looked at Maggie more closely. "Is it working?" he asked.

"Well, I do feel better now that you're here," she told Jonah, taking back her phone and returning it into her pocket.

Jonah put his arm around her shoulders, giving her a quick hug. "Good, that means I've done my job. I'll see if I can find someone at the police department who can track down this coward for me and I'll tell him to back off if *he* knows what's good for *him*," Jonah said, paraphrasing the mysterious caller's initial threat.

"In the meantime," Maggie said, looking over at the frying pan and its semicharred contents, "I burned some chicken for you."

"Mmm, burned chicken. My favorite. How did you know?" he teased.

"Wild guess," she quipped. "No, really," she said, changing her tone. "You don't have to eat it. I'll make you something else."

"Hey, seriously, I really like burned fried food," he assured her. To prove it, he picked up a chicken thigh out of the pan and bit into it. "Hot!" he declared. "But delicious."

# Chapter 12

Maggie looked at the burned fried chicken on the plate that Jonah had taken. She frowned. "You're just saying that," she told him.

"And meaning it," Jonah insisted. "Besides, this chicken is only moderately burned. The skin's just crispy, that's all." He took another healthy bite. The skin crackled as he sank his teeth into the piece. "Turns out that the meat inside is just fine."

"But—" Certain Jonah was just pretending to enjoy the chicken, Maggie began to take the chicken away.

Jonah was not about to relinquish his plate. "Stop arguing with me and let me enjoy my chicken in peace," he told her.

Maggie gave up trying to change his mind. Truthfully, she felt rather relieved that he could actually eat what she'd prepared. The anonymous text she'd gotten had put her in a very strange mood, making her doubt herself and everything else. Having the chicken pieces start smoking and burning only seemed to amplify that feeling.

She had taken a few pieces for herself, but right now, all she was doing was pushing the pieces around on the plate.

About to do justice to his second piece, Jonah saw that Maggie wasn't eating. "Why aren't you having any?" he urged. "I'm betting that you probably haven't had anything to eat since this morning."

She didn't feel up to having Jonah analyze her, so she lied. "I did," Maggie said defensively.

He'd been with her for most of the day. He had a feeling that she hadn't had anything in the short time they had been apart while she'd been making dinner. Still, he was willing to play along and asked, "Okay, what did you have?"

"Food," Maggie answered grudgingly.

Now he knew she was lying, but he wasn't about to come right out and say that. Instead, he asked good-naturedly, "Anything more specific than that?"

"Good food," she answered.

Maggie was prepared to go down fighting, he thought, and it amused him. Jonah started to laugh and wound up laughing so hard that he came close to choking.

Maggie realized that he wasn't kidding. She jumped to her feet and began pounding Jonah on his back. He sucked in his breath. Whatever had gotten caught in his throat had been dislodged.

Holding his hand up, his eyes almost watery, Jonah gasped, "Uncle. I give up." He sucked in more air. "You know, you're a great deal stronger than you look," he told her.

Maggie was still looking at him closely. "Are you all right?" she asked. "You had me worried there for a minute."

He waved away her concern. "Just a little food that went down the wrong way."

She knew that her flippant comment was what had set him off. "I'm sorry," she apologized.

She was kidding, right? "You have nothing to be sorry for. After the kind of day I put in, between finding that body and then digging through more rubble, it felt good to be able to laugh at something." Jonah looked at her for a long moment, his expression growing somber. "There hasn't been all that much to laugh about lately."

Maggie immediately thought of the strange text she had received warning her to back off.

"No, there hasn't been," she agreed. "But we need to hold on to a good thought so that we can move forward. Even when I was up that tree when the floods hit, clinging to that branch for all I was worth, I never thought that was going to be the end for me."

He hadn't even considered that part. He had just assumed that she had been afraid. "Just what did you think?" he asked Maggie.

She smiled at him now. "That's easy. I thought that

someone would come along to save me, and look—" she gestured toward him "—you did."

That surprised him. "You thought *I'd* come and save you?" he questioned.

"Well, not you specifically," she admitted. "But *someone*."

His eyes washed over Maggie and he felt those same stirrings again. There was no doubt about it. He was attracted to Maggie.

Jonah smiled at her. "I guess I'm glad it was me."

"Yeah, me, too," Maggie replied. She saw that Jonah had finished the chicken he had put on his plate. "Can I get you something else?" she asked, about to take the plate from him to throw out the pile of bones.

Something about the way Maggie had asked the question increased those stirrings he was feeling. Attempting to get them under control wasn't working.

"As a matter of fact, there is something else," Jonah answered in a low voice.

"What?"

She'd breathed the word rather than just said it outright. It hung between them like an unspoken, tempting invitation.

Jonah was aware of rising to his feet, his hands on her shoulders, bringing her up with him. The next moment, he leaned in and his lips met hers.

The kiss ignited a host of other things, feelings that had not really faded away but had been hiding just beneath the surface, ready to leap up and seize the moment.

For just a second, his body was sealed to hers. The close proximity woke up every single inch of her.

She wove her arms around his neck, losing herself not just in the kiss but in the man, as well. She could feel her pulse racing, feel herself yearning for more. But that would only be opening up the door for things that might be glorious in the moment, but that undoubtedly came with consequences. Consequences she didn't think she could handle on top of everything else.

With effort, Maggie forced herself to draw her head back. Trying to lighten the moment, she pretended to continue a conversation that hadn't actually gotten underway.

"So you were saying that you'd like some dessert?" she asked.

Understanding why she was doing this, Jonah picked up on her cue. "Yes, but I don't think that there's any available."

"Why don't I just take a look?" Maggie suggested, stepping away. She discreetly took a few deep breaths in an effort to still her erratic pulse as she crossed to the refrigerator. Opening the freezer, she looked in. There wasn't much there. "How do you feel about refrozen ice cream?"

"How's that again?" he asked.

She pulled out a half-filled container of chocolate ice cream. "Refrozen ice cream," she repeated. "It looks like it melted a bit when we lost power, then refroze again when the power came on." She turned the carton around, looking at it from all sides. "I don't think it's bad. At worst, it just probably doesn't taste as good as it should."

Because he was still trying to play along, Jonah turned over the idea of having the ice cream in his mind. "Well, I'm willing to give it a try if you are," he told her.

Maggie hadn't even realized that he had come up behind her just now. She sucked in her breath in surprise as she turned around.

Trying to appear nonchalant, she managed to sound cheerful. "Sure, why not?"

Taking a large spoon, she began scooping out the contents. There was just enough left in the container to provide two decent-sized servings. Maggie divided the chocolate ice cream equally between two bowls and handed one to Jonah.

"Too bad you don't have any whipped cream," she commented, looking down into the bowl.

"I take it that chocolate ice cream isn't your favorite?" Jonah guessed.

Maggie examined the contents again. She wasn't aware of wrinkling her nose just then, but Jonah had taken notice of it.

"It's too chocolaty," she said as they sat down on the couch.

He thought the way she'd wrinkled her nose made her look adorable, but he didn't want to embarrass her, so he kept that to himself.

"Really?" Jonah asked, rather surprised at her answer. "It's my favorite."

"I like mint chip best," Maggie confided.

"That has chocolate in it," Jonah pointed out.

"Yes, but it's not overpowering. It's not *chocolate*," she said, all but shouting out the word to make her point. Looking at her bowl again, she made up her mind. "You know what? You can have mine," she told him, holding out the bowl to him.

"You really don't want it?" Jonah questioned. He was almost finished with the ice cream in his own bowl. Without thinking about it, he had all but inhaled the contents quickly.

"I've had enough," Maggie assured him. "Here. Really," she said, urging him to take the bowl. She glanced at his empty bowl. "I can see that you really do like it."

He placed his empty bowl on the coffee table but instead of taking the one she was offering, Jonah told her, "I do." There was just the slightest dab of chocolate ice cream on the corner of her mouth. "Um, you have a little bit of chocolate right there."

"Where?" she asked, reflexively running her tongue along the upper part of her lip with hopes of clearing away the offending trace. "Here?"

But she hadn't come close to it. "No, right there," he told her.

The next moment, giving in to his urge, Jonah leaned in and removed the tiny dab of ice cream with his own lips. Chocolate ice cream had never tasted this good.

He heard Maggie sighing in contentment against his mouth. That only fanned the flames that had instantly sprung up on contact.

He kissed her again, this time with even more feeling and enthusiasm.

Not wanting to make Maggie feel as if he was attempting to overwhelm her, Jonah forced himself to slowly pull back.

He smiled at Maggie. "No doubt about it," he said. "I really do love chocolate ice cream."

This was her chance to draw away and call it a day. To step back from temptation before she got in over her head and did something she might regret.

To—

*Oh, the hell with it*, Maggie thought, mentally throwing up her hands and giving in. Who was she kidding? They were clearly drawn to one another, why was she trying to resist so hard? The truth of it was she couldn't remember ever being so attracted to a man the way she was to Jonah. Not even to her ex-husband.

Yes, she knew that she didn't have a prayer of this actually going anywhere once this unique scenario was resolved. But they were both here now and maybe, just for a little while, they could enjoy one another without any strings attached.

"You know," she said with a contented sigh, "I think I'm beginning to really change my mind about chocolate ice cream."

"Oh?" he asked, rubbing his finger along her bottom lip, "How so?"

"I'm finding that I'm developing a really strong taste for it," she murmured just as their lips came together again.

All systems were go, but still, Jonah didn't want to take anything for granted. What if he was misreading her signals?

"You're sure about this?" he asked her, giving her a chance to pull away.

She was grateful to him for asking, but at the same time, she didn't want to waste time debating with him.

"I'm sure," she responded. "Now stop talking and let me sample some more of the ice cream that you've managed to get on your mouth."

There was almost a twinkle in her eye, which aroused him.

Everything about her aroused him. There was no use fighting it.

"With pleasure," he told her.

For a moment, as he settled her back into his arms, she thought that Jonah would just take her right then and there, making the most of the moment and her willingness. It was what she was used to, thanks to her ex.

But Jonah surprised her.

He didn't just race to the finish line with her. Instead, he went about making love with her slowly. He began by nibbling on her lips, then moving on to sample other parts of her, gliding his lips along her throat, her shoulders, the soft inviting slope that led down between her breasts.

He made love to her slowly, lyrically, leaving no part of her untouched, unworshipped. He used his lips, his teeth, his hands. Every part of him made love to her.

Maggie tried to keep up, but then she would find herself slipping into the wild, wonderful haven that Jonah was creating for her.

Over and over again, her breath caught in her throat and she would lose her train of thought, lose herself in the wild, wonderful moment that was encompassing her.

He made her forget who she was. *Where* she was. All that existed was this all-consuming fire that he was stoking.

Pulling her blouse from her shoulders and then undoing her bra, letting it slowly sink away from her breasts, Jonah covered her with a fine web of open-mouthed kisses, moving slowly along her throbbing skin.

Jonah was vaguely aware that she was trying to open his belt, fumbling with the clasp. He paused for the slightest moment to undo it for her.

He felt her smile against his skin as he went to kiss her again.

"Always the gentleman," she murmured.

"I do my best," Jonah answered just before he brought his mouth back down to her lips, then to the hollow of her throat.

He reveled in the way her breath was growing louder as well as shorter and shorter in response to what he was doing.

Maggie felt as if her whole body was on fire. She never knew that lovemaking could be this wild, exhilarating experience that had her craving more and more even as it made her want to live in the moment, savoring every second of what was happening.

She was amazed that this experience was so different from what she had experienced before. After all, she'd been married, and James Corgan hadn't exactly been a virgin when he'd taken her. But his expertise for the most part lay in his satisfying himself, not in making love *with* her or *to* her. Compared to Jonah, her ex had been an inept boy. He hadn't been anywhere near the experienced man that Jonah was right at this moment.

Jonah, she realized, seemed dedicated to pleasing her, thereby pleasing himself.

Completely captivated by him, at first Maggie didn't realize that Jonah was carrying her into the bedroom, not until he'd crossed the threshold and was about to place her down on the bed.

This was the way she wanted it to happen, Maggie thought. Not like some tawdry affair, but on a bed like two lovers who had all the time in the world.

The moment she felt the bed against her back, she began to tug on the remainder of his clothing, eager to feel his skin against hers when he drew close to her again. Her fingers flew, as did his, and within moments, they were both as naked as their desire for one another rendered them.

As he began to kiss her over and over again, Maggie firmly wrapped her legs around his torso, holding him to her, urging him to finally consummate their union once and for all.

But still he continued to take his time with her,

despite the fact that he could feel an urgency racing through him. He could feel his eagerness growing by quantum leaps until he just couldn't hold himself in check any longer.

Rolling Maggie onto her back, he drew his body slowly up along hers. He wanted to look into her eyes when they took the final step. But as he balanced himself directly over her, he saw that her eyes were closed.

"Open your eyes, Maggie," he whispered. When they continued to remain closed, he said, "Look at me."

For the first time, just before they became one, she opened her eyes. Her heart was hammering wildly against her chest. She saw Jonah smile down at her and she felt something stirring in response. She had never felt so close to anyone as she felt to Jonah.

And then his knee was nudging her legs apart. Not urgently, as if it was his right, but gently. Her heart melted.

She opened for him and drew in her breath as she felt him entering her. The movement was gentle, not anything like the way James had done it, as if it was his right and she was his property.

The same heart that had melted was swelling now. At this moment—just for this one singular moment—she fell in love with Jonah as he began to move slowly, then more urgently within her.

She met him movement for movement, glorying in their union and eagerly racing toward fulfillment, that wonderful race to the top of the mountain, followed by that breathtaking leap that eventually sent them spiraling downward.

She dug her fingers into his shoulders as they took the leap together.

# Chapter 13

Though he tried to hold on to it as long as he could, Jonah found that the euphoria between them receded all too soon. As he listened to her breathing become steadier, quieter, Jonah leaned in and pressed a kiss to the top of her head.

Maggie stirred and stretched against him, then turned to look up at him quizzically.

She appeared just as stunned as he felt. Smiling, he gently swept her hair out of her face. "That was a surprise," he told her.

Maggie drew herself up on her elbow and gazed at him, bemused. "Did you expect me to start throwing things at you?"

"No, of course not," he responded, searching his brain for the right way to put his thoughts into words.

"I just didn't expect…" His voice trailed off and then he finally said, "for all this to happen."

"And now you're regretting it?" she guessed, bracing herself for the disappointment she knew would come if he hinted at that.

Jonah's dark eyebrows drew together in utter confusion that she should think something like that.

"Oh hell no," he told Maggie. "I just didn't want you to feel overwhelmed—" That didn't come out right. "I mean—"

She smiled at him. He was concerned that he had imposed his will on her, she realized. The man was incredibly sweet.

"I know what you mean," she said, stopping him. "And trust me, Jonah, if I didn't want this to happen, it wouldn't have. I know how to take care of myself, and you," she emphasized with a grin, "don't strike me as being a Neanderthal."

"I'm not," he agreed with feeling.

Her eyes smiled before her mouth even began to curve. "I know."

"So you're okay with what happened?" Jonah asked, searching her face and wanting to be totally sure that they really were on the same page.

"I'm better than okay," Maggie assured him, snuggling up in the crook of his arm.

Jonah grinned. "Well, in that case…" His voice trailed off provocatively.

She raised herself up on her elbow again, tantalized by what she heard in his voice. "Just what did you have in mind?"

The expression in his eyes was positively nothing short of wicked. "Guess," he challenged.

Her pulse sped up again, going into double time. "You'll have to give me a hint," she teased.

Jonah leaned in and kissed her, a wave of unbridled passion beginning to churn within him in a matter of seconds. It was hard to hold himself in check.

She was practically breathless when he drew his lips away. Taking a second to collect herself, Maggie whispered, "I'm going to need more of a hint than that."

He pulled her to him, her back sliding along the sheets.

"More of a hint coming up," he told her just before he sealed his mouth over hers again.

How could it be dawn already?

Maggie opened her eyes warily, hoping she was imagining things. But she wasn't. Daylight was skimming along the floor in the cabin bedroom. She felt as if she had gotten less than three hours sleep.

Trying to be quiet, Maggie slipped out of bed, her whole body still humming from the activities of just a few hours ago. Quickly collecting her clothes, she got dressed in the living area. Her plan was to make coffee, maybe even breakfast if Jonah had enough eggs left in the refrigerator.

After that, she'd see where the day took them.

She had just managed to crack four eggs and deposit them into the frying pan when Jonah tiptoed up behind her, slipping his arms around her waist and giving her a quick hug.

Kissing her neck, he told her, "I would have made breakfast."

She tried not to shiver as the kiss zipped along her sensitive skin.

"It's my turn," she reminded him.

He laughed, releasing her. "I would have thought after last night, you would be too tired to get up and cook."

She gave him a side glance. His shirt was hanging open with a tempting view of his muscular chest. Maggie ordered herself to focus.

"The same would go for you, wouldn't it?" she asked, scrambling the eggs.

Stepping back, Jonah started to put out the utensils to set the table. "I'm used to getting by on very little sleep and putting in a long day."

"So you're telling me that you do this sort of thing all the time?" she asked, tongue in cheek.

"Yes—no," he quickly corrected, realizing what she was saying. "I mean—"

Delighted, Maggie laughed. He looked adorable when he was flustered. "I'd quit while I was ahead if I were you, Jonah," she advised. The toast popped just then. She nodded toward the toaster. "Why don't you make yourself useful and butter the toast?" she suggested with a straight face.

Jonah nodded. "I should butter the toast," he agreed. Dropping the four slices onto a plate, he took out the butter and began to spread it generously across each of the four surfaces.

Maggie laughed. Good-looking, good-natured and a fantastic lover, the man really was a rare combination. She told herself not to think any further than today.

"You realize I'm giving you a hard time, don't you?" she asked.

"I'm tough," he declared, deliberately keeping a serious face. "I can take it."

"Oh, but you do have a very soft center," she said wistfully, allowing herself to drift back to last night just for a moment.

"I'd rather we keep that just between us," he told her.

She wondered if that gave her an exclusive edge. She decided not to explore that thought too closely. "Consider it done," she replied.

Dividing the scrambled eggs between the two plates, she placed two pieces of the toast he'd buttered on each plate and then handed him one plate while she took the other.

"I've been thinking," Maggie said, taking her seat opposite him.

"When?" Jonah asked in all innocence. They'd made love almost all night and then when he woke up, he'd found her in the kitchen, busy with breakfast. The woman was a whirlwind. "When did you have time to think?"

Maggie grinned, knowing exactly what Jonah was referring to.

"I multitask," she told him. With a wink she added, "I can do at least two things at once."

She was telling him that her mind was whirling even as they were making love last night. "I don't know if I should be impressed or insulted," he told her.

"Flattered," she corrected. "You should be flattered because you're an inspiration and you were the one who got all my juices flowing."

Well, put that way, he couldn't be insulted that her mind was elsewhere. "And exactly what is it that you were thinking about?"

Maggie smiled like a woman who knew she was about to drop a bombshell. And then she did. "I think we should go and pay Elliott Corgan a visit."

Jonah's fork froze just as he brought it up to his mouth. He looked at her as if she had slipped a gear. "You want to go and visit the serial killer?"

Maggie nodded. Swallowing what she had put in her mouth, she said, "One and the same."

"But the man's in prison," Jonah protested. Had she forgotten that?

"I know. But I think we need to talk to him," she insisted. Now that she knew all about the "family secret," she had questions she wanted to ask James's uncle. "He might be the only one who could tell us what happened to the chief's sister."

"Thompson said he talked to Elliott and the man denied killing her," Jonah reminded her, finishing his eggs.

"And serial killers are always so truthful," she responded sarcastically.

Jonah frowned. She had a point. "You're serious about wanting to talk to Elliott?" he questioned.

Finished with her own meal, she wiped her mouth, then dropped her napkin onto the plate. "Absolutely."

He could see that she was serious, but that still didn't make this doable. "And we're just going to waltz up to that prison in Austin and ask to see Elliott Corgan," he asked incredulously.

"No," she said simply, "we can drive. Waltzing will take too much time."

"Very funny," he responded, then rephrased his question. "And we just walk into Randolph State Prison and ask to see him, out of the blue. What makes you think we can pull that off? Or that we can even get him to talk to us?"

Though she had only come up with this while making breakfast, she had given it a lot of thought.

"Well, technically, I am family, so to speak. I'm his nephew's former wife. More importantly," she stressed, "the man's a serial killer. Once they're caught, they revel in attention, in showing everyone how much more clever they are than everyone else."

He could almost see her mind figuring out the details. He was in awe of the way it worked.

"We can tell Elliott that we're true crime documentarians and that we're interested in bringing his story to the small screen. Once he knows that, we probably won't be able to get him to *stop* talking," she said confidently.

He still wasn't sold on the idea. "Thompson told us to stay clear of this. Again," Jonah reminded her.

She sighed. "I know, but you can't tell me that he doesn't want to know who's responsible for his sister's death."

"I'm sure he does," Jonah conceded, "but Thompson's perfectly capable of going to question Elliot himself if he wanted to do that."

"He already did," she reminded Jonah. "That's how the chief knows that Elliot denied having anything to do with Emmeline's death," she said, paraphrasing what Jonah had just said earlier.

Jonah saw the look on Maggie's face. She was determined to do this, he thought. "But you don't believe him," he guessed.

"Let's just say I need to be convinced of Elliott's innocence in this case. After all, he *is* the likely killer," she pointed out.

Jonah felt as if they were going around in circles. "Again, if there is something to pursue, Thompson's the one who should do it."

She agreed, but there was a glaring problem with that. "He's a police chief. His hands are tied by rules and regulations."

Jonah eyed her, rather bemused. "And ours aren't?"

Maggie smiled at him. "Let's just say that for us, the rules and regulations are bendable." Picking up the empty plates, she piled the utensils on top and took everything to the sink. "You don't have to say anything," she told him. "I can do all the talking. You can just be there as my backup. Or my cameraman," she said, really beginning to get enthusiastic about the idea.

"Don't get carried away," he warned. He knew someone who had tried to make a film on the premises and had gotten stymied. "There are all sorts of forms to fill out if you want to bring a camera onto prison grounds. That'll take time to get clearance and I can see by the look on your face that you're dying to just jump in and do this thing."

"Okay, no camera," she told him, perfectly willing to adjust her plan to fit the situation. "You can just be there to take notes."

He made a calculated guess. "So you'll be the producer."

"Hey, it's my idea, right?" Maggie reminded him with a grin.

"And if I said that it's not a good idea?" Jonah challenged.

She wasn't about to force him to go with her. "All right, you don't have to come. I'll go by myself," she told Jonah.

If she thought he was about to go along with that, she didn't know him at all. He had absolutely no intention of letting Maggie go into the prison by herself. "The hell you will."

Inwardly, she breathed a sigh of relief, then smiled at him. "The offer's still open to be my sidekick," she told Jonah.

"You are incorrigible, you know that, don't you?" he said, shaking his head.

"Oh, I might have heard that before," Maggie conceded.

He laughed dryly. "'With good reason, I'm sure." He saw that Maggie had opened her mouth, a clear sign that she was about to share a story with him, most likely about the last time she had been called incorrigible.

"Wait," he spoke up before she could get started, "I don't want to know."

There was humor in her eyes. "Your loss," Maggie said glibly.

"That is a matter of opinion," Jonah countered with feeling. He thought for a moment, doing some mental juggling. "I'm going to have to go by the latest rescue site to find out if I can be spared today," he told her.

This was turning out to involve a lot of logistics, she thought. "I said I can go alone," Maggie reminded him.

Jonah had made up his mind. There was no way he wanted her to see that killer without protection. "The hell you can."

She looked at him for a long moment. For once, Jonah couldn't begin to guess what Maggie was thinking.

"You realize that you can't order me around, don't you?" she asked.

"I saved your life," Jonah reminded her. "In some cultures, that means your life belongs to me. If it belongs to me, I get to have a say about where it goes or doesn't go."

Her eyes narrowed as she tried to discern whether he was joking not. "Are you serious?"

"No," he admitted. "But it was worth a shot. However, if you insist on doing something stupid and try to take off without me, I'm within my rights to handcuff you to my bed until you start thinking clearly."

"You wouldn't dare," she told him, unconsciously sticking out her chin.

"I wouldn't go betting anything on that if I were you, Maggie," he told her, his tone so serious that she wasn't sure if he was putting her on or not. "I'm just asking for a couple of hours. You can come with me," he added.

She sighed. "I guess I can do that," she responded.

Admittedly, she wasn't all that happy about this delay, necessary though it was from his viewpoint. Now that she had come up with a plan, she wanted to be out there, implementing it. If pressed, she couldn't exactly explain why, but she had this sense of urgency vibrating within her, as if she felt that she only had a limited amount of time to get to the truth before it would be lost to her forever.

Maggie supposed that the hurricane was partially responsible for creating that feeling. Having watched the giant funnel rip through buildings that had seemed so solid looking one minute, only to become a pile of rubble and wood the next made her feel that everything could come apart with a second's notice, burying vital answers forever.

"All right, you have a deal. Just let me finish washing the dishes and I'll go with you. But you have to promise me that barring another hurricane—or flash flood—we are going to go to Austin to see Elliott Corgan—"

"Your former uncle-in-law," he acknowledged.

"Well, I didn't know that at the time," Maggie confessed. "I never met the man and no one in the family ever told me about him."

"Small wonder. If you'd known, you might have opted out of the wedding," Jonah guessed.

She would have liked to have agreed with him, but she couldn't, not without lying about it.

"Actually," Maggie admitted, "I couldn't. I had obligations and the only way I knew how to meet them was to marry James."

"You married him for his money?" he asked her. That didn't sound like her, but then, how much did he really know about Maggie?

"No, I married him because I loved him, but I'd be lying if I said that the money was of absolutely no consequence to me. I needed the money to help my parents the only way I knew how," she admitted. "They were drowning in medical bills and needed help. By marrying James, I could provide that help. Unfortunately," she said sadly, "I wasn't able to do it before they died."

"That must have been really disappointing for you," he said.

"It was." She roused herself. There was no point in dwelling on the past. "So I used the money to buy Bellamy our old family home. I didn't want to have anything to do with the money," she said passionately. "Having it made me feel cheap."

"*Cheap* is the last word I would associate with you," Jonah told her as he locked the door to his cabin.

She really was something else, he couldn't help thinking. The more he knew about her, the more he found to like.

## Chapter 14

Jonah felt torn.

Because of the amount of damage created by the hurricane and the subsequent flooding, he felt it was his duty to remain in Whisperwood so he could help with the cleanup efforts. At this point, it was no longer a search and rescue operation. Whoever might still be buried beneath all the debris was most likely dead.

But just because there were no more rescues to head up, that didn't mean that there wasn't work to be done. The nature of this work involved digging up whatever bodies might still be buried under all that havoc caused by the storm, plus clearing everything else away so that the rebuilding could begin.

But although his sense of duty urged him to stay and work alongside his team, a far greater sense of loyalty had him wanting to accompany Maggie to the Austin state prison. He knew she couldn't be talked out of trying to get to the bottom of the riddle that her late former father-in-law had sent to her via his lawyer. She was stubborn that way.

There were others on the team who could take his place and do the work that was needed, but as far as he was concerned, there was no one available to go with Maggie, so his choice was clear.

The way he saw it, he didn't *have* a choice. He had to go with Maggie. Not just to be beside her when she walked through the prison gates, but also because of the anonymous text threat she'd received.

Jonah supposed that the latter could just be a stupid prank, but his gut told him it wasn't. It was something he had to take seriously. Otherwise, if he just ignored it, he had a feeling that he would regret it.

And worse than that, Maggie might just wind up regretting it. That sealed the argument for him.

So, less than an hour after they had left his cabin, he and Maggie were on the road, driving toward Randolph State Prison in Austin.

But he had to admit that he still felt uneasy about the venture.

"You sure you want to do this?" Jonah asked her when they were about twenty minutes into their trip to the prison. "It's not too late just to turn around and go back."

"It's not exactly a destination I'd pick out for a fun road trip, but yes," Maggie answered, "I'm sure—

because there is no other way around this. No stone unturned, right?"

He didn't quite see it that way. "You know, there's no shame in just abandoning this whole thing. It's not up to you to find the answers," he pointed out.

A smile slowly curved her mouth. "You don't know me very well, otherwise you wouldn't say that. I don't abandon things," she told him with pride. "I see them through."

He blew out an impatient breath. "I'll make sure they put that on your tombstone."

If he was being sarcastic, she wasn't buying into it. "There are worse things to have on a tombstone," she told him glibly.

Jonah gave up trying to convince her to let him turn the truck back. He knew if he did, she would only set out for the prison on her own the first chance she got. While he liked the fact that Maggie was brave and determined, there was such a thing as being *too* brave and *too* determined. In his opinion, that was only asking for trouble and they already had enough of that, thanks to the hurricane.

He went on to a more immediate problem. "Okay, we're almost there. You still want to go through with this supposed documentary filmmakers ruse?"

"Sure," she answered. She saw the doubtful look on Jonah's face. "It beats pretending that we're some kind of ghoulish groupies or fans. I hear that a lot of mass murderers have them." Even as she said it, Maggie couldn't help shivering at the improbable thought. "I will never be able to understand people like that."

"That's because you're normal," Jonah told her simply. He took in a long breath. They were approaching the massive prison gates. Even in broad daylight, the prison looked foreboding. "Okay, time to take out our IDs," he prompted. "Remember, these prison guards are always on the lookout for any kind of suspicious behavior. Randolph State Prison hasn't had a successful prison break in the last forty years."

"I hope that doesn't mean they're overdue for one," Maggie murmured, feeling progressively less secure the closer they came to the gates.

"Positive thoughts, remember?" Jonah found it ironic that he was reminding Maggie of the basic philosophy that she espoused.

"Right," Maggie mumbled under her breath, taking out her wallet. She passed it over to Jonah just as he pulled his truck up next to the guard.

"Well, that wasn't the least bit intimidating," Maggie commented as they were waved on through the gates several long minutes later.

"Actually," Jonah told her as they drove through the parking lot, searching for a space, "as far as these sorts of things go, this was rather laid-back and routine," he told her.

"Laid-back, huh?" she questioned. "Remind me to live an exemplary life once we get out of here," Maggie cracked.

"Remember, you were the one who wanted to come here," he told her.

"I know, I know," Maggie answered. "You're right. And I don't regret this," she wanted him to know. "I'm just going to need a long hot shower once we get back home," she said.

*Home.* She had just referred to his cabin as home, Jonah thought. He wondered if she even realized that, or if she'd thought of it as a mistake the second the words were out of her mouth?

He eyed her, but there was no change in Maggie's expression and he wasn't going to be the one who brought it to her attention.

For all he knew, she'd meant it. Maybe she had actually started to think of his cabin as "home." Jonah turned the idea over in his head. He didn't know if he felt uncomfortable about that—or if he was actually rather pleased.

And then, suddenly, there was no longer any time left to contemplate anything. They had left the truck behind them and were now about to walk through the prison doors.

*Showtime.*

"I think that by the time we leave here, our IDs are going to be worn-out," Maggie commented as they followed a prison guard to a general gathering area where prisoners were allowed to meet with family members and friends. By her count, they had produced their IDs four times since approaching the prison gates—and then had to surrender them as well as their cell phones at the last station.

"That's probably the general idea," Jonah replied. He saw her looking at him in confusion, so he explained. "Fake IDs don't stand up to all that handling, at least the poor ones don't," he amended.

Maggie shrugged, at a loss. "I know you know what you're talking about, but I'm not really sure I understand that," she confessed.

Just then, before Jonah could explain it to her more clearly, Maggie grabbed his hand, holding on to him very tightly.

Her eyes were riveted on the scrawny, mangy-looking man with the unruly gray hair. He was wearing an orange jumpsuit and being escorted in by not just one guard, but two, one positioned on either side of him.

Elliott Corgan was just a shade smaller than his two uniformed bookends, not to mention a good deal older. But neither time, nor size could subdue the very menacing shadow that the man cast just by his mere presence in a room, no matter how large that room was.

The sharp, almost-black eyes moved around the area, taking in everything at once.

Even now, as old as he was, Maggie had the feeling that Elliott Corgan was not a man she could safely turn her back on.

When one of the guards pointed toward Jonah and her, Maggie could feel her throat closing up a little. And when Elliott stared in her direction, his small, marble-like eyes honing in on her even at that distance, for just a moment, Maggie thought she was going to be sick.

Sheer will had her keeping her breakfast down. Maggie refused to give Corgan the satisfaction of knowing he had intimidated her.

Noting her pallor, Jonah leaned in and whispered, "We can still leave."

But she was adamant. "No, we've come this far, I'm not about to turn tail and run now," she told him fiercely. A little more fiercely than she was actually feeling at the moment.

Drawing her shoulders back, Maggie released her death grip on his hand and made her way toward an empty table.

Jonah was right beside her, intent on being her body-guard. He didn't like the way that Elliott Corgan was looking at her, as if he was sizing her up, no doubt just the way the man had sized up his victims all those years ago.

This was a bad idea.

Elliott put his hand on the back of the chair, claim-ing it. He sat down opposite them.

Prison hadn't broken him, Jonah thought. Instead, Corgan held himself erect like a man who was confi-dent in the fact that he was feared and thus respected in the warped world where he resided.

The intense dark eyes passed quickly over him, but it was Maggie who seemed to interest Corgan.

Corgan devoured her with his eyes.

Maggie had to struggle in order not to shiver or to allow the revulsion she felt toward the prisoner to show through. If Corgan saw contempt in her eyes, she knew he wouldn't be inclined to cooperate.

He still might not be, she thought. But she had to try.

Corgan was first to speak. "Who are you?"

Lies were best if they were kept simple—she had heard that somewhere. So she gave the convicted serial killer their real names.

"I'm Maggie Reeves." She nodded toward Jonah as she completed the introduction. "And this is Jonah Colton. We've come to get your side of the story and present it to our audience."

A flicker of interest rose in Elliott's dark eyes. He stared at her intently. "You two are saying that you're filmmakers?" he questioned.

Maggie raised her head, refusing to look away, refusing to be intimidated. She met his gaze head-on. "Yes," Maggie answered proudly.

Elliott smirked at the duo sitting before him. "You ain't no such thing," he snarled in a superior tone. "You're frauds and you're wasting my time," he told them, pushing the chair back as he began to rise.

"Seems to me that you've got nothing but time," Jonah told him. His gaze was unwavering even though being so close to Corgan literally turned his stomach. But this was important to Maggie so he pressed on. "Don't you want to know why we're really here?" he asked the man serving several life sentences.

Elliot sat down again. His eyes lingered on Maggie before he said to Jonah, "Okay, I'll bite. Who are you two and what the hell are you doing here?"

Maggie spoke up. "I already gave you our names," she told him, then added, "I used to be married to your nephew, James." She watched the serial killer as the information sank in.

The thin cheeks spread in a chilling, lecherous

smile. "Well, come here, darlin', and let me give you a hug to welcome you into the family," Corgan told her, rising again. The chair scraped along the floor as he pushed it back.

He leaned over the table, his arms spread out toward Maggie.

The guard, who had remained in the doorway watching Corgan, was instantly alert and crossed the room to the prisoner.

"Hey, you know the rules. No contact," the guard barked at him.

The latter raised his hands in mock submission. "No contact," Corgan repeated in a scornful voice. Then he looked at his visitors. "They're afraid if I touch someone, they'll wind up dead," he chuckled, amused by his own joke. "You're not afraid of me, are you, darlin'?" Corgan asked, leering at Maggie.

"Why don't we get down to business?" Jonah said in a cold, stern voice.

"I'm always all about business." Corgan's thin lips pulled back in a sneer as he looked at Maggie again.

Maggie had planned to approach her questioning slowly, but obviously this wasn't a man who responded to subtlety. He had to be all but beaten over the head with questions.

So rather than find the right way to ask, she just forged ahead and asked her questions. "We found Emmeline Thompson's body the other day. She was buried beneath that really huge oak on your brother's ranch," she told Corgan, watching his face for any sort of a reaction.

Corgan's drawn face remained impassive. "Do tell." He leaned in over the table, stopped just short of making contact. "Why don't you refresh my memory, darlin'?"

"You should remember this one," Maggie all but spit out. "You mummified her and wrapped her up in plastic." To her horror, Corgan began to laugh. She exchanged looks with Jonah.

"What are you laughing at, you pervert?" Jonah demanded.

"Emmeline Thompson," Corgan repeated with a chilling smile. "I remember."

Maggie looked alert. "You remember killing her?" she cried.

"No, I remember really *wishing* I had done her." Corgan looked up, making eye contact with Maggie. "But I can't take the credit for that." He spread his hands out. "I'm innocent."

"You've never known an innocent day in your life," Jonah snarled at the man.

Corgan inclined his head, conceding the point. "Maybe so, but I'm innocent of killing the Thompson girl. Don't get me wrong, I'd love to add another kill to my list, but I can't because I didn't touch her." And then he looked at Maggie, his interest aroused. "Did you say she was mummified?"

Maggie found it extremely difficult not to shout at the lowlife scum sitting right in front of her. "You know she was."

Corgan shook his head. "Like I said, it wasn't me. But you saying that she was mummified, well, that

gives me an idea about who actually did do the deed."
He smiled mysteriously.

That was when the prison guard came up to the
table again. "Time's up, Corgan," the burly man announced.

"Who was it?" Maggie asked as Corgan got up
from the table. "Who killed Emmeline?" she asked
him urgently.

Corgan was obviously enjoying this. "Well, if I'm
right, that guy's still out there, probably killing more
young women. Maybe even as we're all standing in
here, talking about him."

"Who?" Maggie demanded, her voice rising. "Who
is it?"

"Hey, I'm not going to tell you again, Corgan," the
guard growled at him.

"Sorry, you heard the guard." Corgan was enjoying
himself now. "I've gotta go," he told the two people
questioning him with relish. "But y'all come back
and visit me real soon now, you hear? Maybe I'll tell
you who it is then," Corgan tossed over his shoulder,
relishing this game that he was playing with them.
"You know where to find me. I'm not going to be
going anywhere for a long, long time."

Corgan paused one last second in the doorway, just
leering at Maggie, before the guard roughly pulled
him away.

Since their meeting had been abruptly terminated,
Maggie and Jonah got up to leave. Another guard was
there to make sure they didn't linger.

When they stopped to get their personal possessions

from the guard in charge of holding on to them, Maggie turned toward Jonah and asked, "Think he's telling the truth? That he knows who's responsible for Emmeline's death?"

Reunited with his phone and his watch, Jonah put them into his pockets. "Ordinarily, I'd say no, that Corgan just said that to mess with your head. But there was a look that came into his eyes when you mentioned that the chief's sister was mummified and wrapped up in plastic."

"What kind of look?" Maggie asked, because she had totally missed it.

"Surprised. Like this was news to him. And then he brightened up," Jonah continued as they made their way down the corridor and to the first exit, "like he suddenly made a connection. The man just might be a consummate actor, and given that he got away with all those murders for so long, he could be, but my gut tells me that maybe, just maybe, we caught Corgan off his game for a second. He really looked surprised by the details of Emmeline's murder."

Passing through another doorway, they finally made their way outside. "So that means Corgan *does* know who did it."

Jonah nodded. "And if there's a chance that he does, our next step is to tell the chief."

"You're right," Maggie agreed.

He grinned. "Finally."

## Chapter 15

They were almost back in Whisperwood when Maggie's cell phone buzzed, announcing that she had received another text message.

Jonah glanced at her. "Maybe that's your sister with an update on the wedding," he said hopefully.

Hurricane Brooke had forced everyone's plans to be placed temporarily on hold and that included Donovan and Bellamy's wedding. But the rec center, which was where the reception was to be held, had miraculously avoided being on the receiving end of any damages, major or minor. With all the people who had initially been invited to the wedding slowly getting their lives back in order, things were looking up. It seemed to Jonah that all that needed to be done at this point was to decide on a new date and then proceed with the actual wedding.

With that thought foremost in her mind, Maggie pulled out her phone, entered her passcode and swiped open the message center.

When she didn't say anything, Jonah looked in her direction.

Maggie's expression was grim.

Red flags immediately went up. "I take it from the look on your face that the text you just got isn't from Bellamy."

"No," Maggie answered quietly, "it's not."

The next second, she pressed the home button, causing the message she'd just read to disappear.

"Who is it from?" Jonah asked, although as far as he was concerned, it was a rhetorical question. The tone of her voice had told him everything.

"I don't know." It was the truth. She didn't, and the fact that she didn't both exasperated and frightened her.

"You received another anonymous text?" Jonah asked, already making that assumption. He waited for Maggie to fill him in on the details.

Maggie shrugged, looking out the side window. "It doesn't matter."

"Yes, it does," Jonah insisted. He abruptly pulled his truck over to the side of the road, pulling up the handbrake. As the truck idled, he turned in his seat to look at Maggie. "It was from that same person again, wasn't it?"

She sighed, still staring out the window. "It looks that way."

"Let me see it," Jonah said, holding his hand out and waiting.

Although she was far from happy about it, Maggie surrendered her cell phone to him.

Jonah found himself looking down at a dark screen. Handing it back to her, he said, "Nice try, Maggie. Type in your passcode."

Reluctantly, she typed it in, then pulled up the last text message that had just come in from the anonymous sender. She gave the cell phone back to Jonah. He read aloud.

I warned you to back off if you want to live.

He looked at Maggie. "He gets right to the point, doesn't he?"

"Don't worry about it," she told Jonah, slipping her phone back into her pocket. "I said it's just a stupid prank."

"I *am* worried about it because it's not a stupid prank," Jonah insisted. "Once is a prank," he told her, "twice is a pattern. Best-case scenario, somebody wants to scare you off. Worst case—we don't want to think about worst case."

"You think this is somehow connected to Emmeline Thompson's death?" she asked him.

He didn't need to think about it to answer. "Well, it's a hell of a coincidence if it's not. You got the first text from this guy after you went 'exploring' in the middle of a hurricane—"

"The hurricane hadn't hit when I went out to the

ranch," she reminded Jonah with a touch of defensiveness.

He gave her a look that clearly told her he thought she was splitting hairs.

"And this latest text came just after you went to visit Corgan in prison to question him about the body we found," Jonah said.

"You think we're being watched?" she asked, forcing herself to put her fear into words.

What he was worried about was that *she* was being watched, but he didn't want to state it that way because he didn't want to scare Maggie any more than he had to. He felt it was better to stick with the pronoun she had used.

"That would be my guess," he said. "Maybe the chief has an IT person who could backtrack this text message to a specific phone."

Maggie nodded, agreeing. "Then I guess we have two reasons to see the chief," she said. She pointed toward his idling engine. "You're wasting gas, you know. Let's go."

Amusement came into his eyes. "Yes, ma'am," Jonah responded easily.

Her eyebrows drew together over flashing blue eyes. "Call me 'ma'am' again and that'll be the last word you ever get to say."

This time Jonah laughed. "Information duly noted, Ms. Reeves." He pulled back onto the road. "Now let's go find the chief."

They lucked out and found Chief Thompson as the latter was heading back to his office. He gave the appearance of someone who had been out working all day. He also looked far from happy.

"What the hell's wrong with people?" he complained the moment they caught up with him and managed to get his attention.

"I've got a strong feeling that you're about to tell us," Jonah guessed.

Thompson didn't appear to even hear him. If he did, he didn't comment on Jonah's attempt to infuse humor into the serious situation.

"Don't get me wrong," Thompson said. "Most of these folks are out there helping one another and that's how it should be."

"But?" Jonah asked, waiting for the chief to get to the end of his thought and tell them what was bothering him.

"But then I find two of our younger citizens who should know better looting. Looting!" he repeated with disgust. "They were taking advantage of this catastrophe and making off with things other Whisperwood residents could put to use." His eyes blazed as he shook his head. "If I live to be a hundred, I will never understand that sort of behavior," he declared angrily.

"These sorts of disasters bring out the worst in some people, but they also bring out the best in others and usually the latter outweighs the former," Maggie told the older man, hoping that might restore his usually even temperament. They needed him clearheaded.

"I know, I know," Thompson answered, still disgruntled. "It's just that the former leaves a really bad taste in my mouth."

The chief shook his head again, unlocking his door and walking into his unoccupied office. His other officers were out in the field, helping out and doing whatever needed to be done.

"Well, we have some news, Chief, that may or may not cheer you up," Jonah told Thompson, watching the older man's face.

Gripping the armrests, Thompson eased his large frame onto his office chair. The way he did it indicated that this was the first time he'd sat down all day. "I'm listening," he practically bit off.

Jonah looked at Maggie, indicating that, for better or for worse, this was her story to relate. So she took over. "Jonah and I drove over to Austin to see Elliott Corgan at Randolph State Prison this morning."

Thompson received the news with all the joy of being on the receiving end of a gut punch. He scowled at the two people before him.

"Damn it, I told you two to stay clear of this case! Why the hell didn't you listen?" he demanded.

"It's not his fault, Chief. I insisted on going and Jonah didn't want me to go alone," she said, looking toward Jonah before continuing. "I thought if I could confront Corgan, I could get him to tell me if he killed your sister."

"And what did he say?" the chief asked, his expression dark.

Maggie took a breath. "He said he didn't do it."

"Big surprise," Thompson commented sarcastically. "Of course he'd deny it. I already told you he denied it when I questioned him," the chief reminded the two people in his office.

"I know," Maggie replied. "But it was the way that he denied it. Like he really wished he could have been the one to have done the deed."

"Sick bastard," the chief muttered under his breath in total disgust.

"But that's not all," Jonah said, injecting his own take on the interview with the serial killer. "When Maggie described the way your sister was buried, that her body was mummified first, Corgan got this look on his face, like he suddenly had a revelation."

The chief seemed to come to attention, his whole body growing rigid. "What kind of a revelation?"

It was Maggie's turn to speak. "I think he might know who did kill your sister."

Thompson looked at her doubtfully. "You sure you're not just reading things into this?" he questioned, looking from Maggie to Jonah.

"Very sure," Maggie answered. "Elliott really enjoys being the center of attention. He likes having an audience and right now, he's drawing his story out, baiting us until he finally finds the right moment to reveal his information."

"And you think he's going to tell you who this other killer is?" the chief questioned.

"Yes," Jonah answered. There was no mistaking his confidence.

"Well then, let's go," Thompson urged, rising up from his chair.

"I think we should be the ones to go back and talk to him," Jonah told the chief. "He shut you out once," he reminded Thompson. "But I get the feeling that he likes bragging and preening in front of Maggie."

"Must me my fatal charm," Maggie said sarcastically. She wasn't happy about Corgan's attraction to her, but she was determined to use it to her advantage.

The chief didn't look overly happy about this revelation, even though he didn't contest it.

Resigned, he said, "Fine, then the two of you go back and see him tomorrow morning. It doesn't matter who gets the truth out of him as long as the truth does come out. But the minute you leave that cold-blooded scumbag, I want you to report everything he told you back to me. Am I making myself clear?" Thompson asked, his steely gaze shifting from Maggie to Jonah and then back again.

"Crystal," Maggie answered.

"Um, chief, there is just one more thing," Jonah said as Thompson was about to turn his back on them and get to the paperwork he absolutely dreaded.

Thompson's eyes rose to pin Jonah down. He leaned in closer. "Yes?"

"Maggie's been getting threatening texts on her phone lately," Jonah told the chief.

"Is this true?" Thompson asked her.

She really wished Jonah hadn't said anything, but she had no choice. She had to answer in the affirmative. "Yes. But there've only been two," she protested as if that made it all right.

Thompson's complexion flushed. "Why didn't you come to me with this, Maggie?"

She gestured toward his desk as if it was a symbol for the whole town and what he was carrying on his shoulders.

"Well, it's not as if you didn't already have your hands full," she pointed out.

The chief didn't bother dignifying her excuse with a comment. "Do you have any idea who might have sent them?" he asked her.

Maggie shook her head. "Not a clue."

"That's why we brought this to you," Jonah explained. He held his hand out for the phone. Maggie reluctantly surrendered it. "We thought maybe your IT person could track the texts back to their source."

"He could," the chief agreed, his mouth set grimly, "except for one small problem."

"And that is?" Jonah asked.

"Jim Ellis, my IT person, was one of Hurricane Brooke's casualties," he told them. "The first, actually," he confessed unhappily.

Maggie was the first one to react. "I'm so very sorry for your loss, Chief."

"Yeah, we all are," the chief told her. "Jim was one of those eager beavers who came in early, stayed late and never walked away until he had finished his job. He was really good at it, too."

"Did Jim have a family?" Maggie asked sympathetically.

"No, but he was hoping for one," he told her. "Jim was engaged," he explained, then added sadly, "I was the one who had to break the news to his fiancée." He looked at them with a very sober expression on his face. "There are times when I really hate this job."

And then he focused not on the news that they had brought him about his sister, but on Maggie's threatening texts.

"Let me see your phone," he said to her.

Maggie put in her passcode, then pulled up the two texts for the chief to look at.

"And you got these when?" he asked after reading each one.

"One came in just after we got back from finding your sister's body, the other one came today after we got back from seeing Corgan at the prison."

"Did you tell anyone about going to see Corgan?" he asked.

"No one," Jonah answered for her.

"Did you notice anyone following you?" he asked them.

"The aftermath of the hurricane has people milling around all over the place," Maggie told the chief. "I never took notice of anyone in particular, but that's not to say that someone *wasn't* deliberately following us," she said.

"We're kind of shorthanded right now, otherwise I'd assign someone to protect you around the clock," the chief said almost apologetically.

Jonah cleared his throat. "In case you didn't notice, Chief, I'm here. I can provide Maggie with all the protection and care she might need to keep her safe and sound from this maniac who's trying to scare her off by texting."

The chief looked at him skeptically, but when he spoke, he said, "Well then, I guess there's nothing to worry about, is there?"

"Are you being sarcastic?" Jonah asked him good-naturedly.

"No, but I am reminded of that old saying. You know the one I mean. It's the one about the best-laid plans of mice and men," the chief answered.

"Okay, you *are* being sarcastic," Jonah concluded.

"Well, don't be. Search and rescue aren't the only things I'm trained in," he assured the chief.

Maggie raised her hand to draw attention to herself and away from a possible brewing dispute. "I'm right here and although I am touched that you're both concerned about keeping me safe. I am perfectly capable of doing that myself."

"No one's arguing with that," Jonah told her, "but there is that other old saying," he said, taking a page out of the chief's book, "about two heads being better than one. That goes for protectors, as well," he told Maggie in no uncertain terms.

She smiled at him. "Seeing as how it's me you're trying to keep safe, I'm not going to argue with that."

Jonah looked at her. He knew there was more coming. "But?"

"No 'but,'" she said innocently. "However, didn't you say if we got back early, you wanted to lend a hand in the cleanup efforts?"

He thought that in light of the text, things had changed. "I did, but—"

Maggie pretended not to hear his protest. "Well then, let's go, Colton," she ordered. "We're standing around, wasting daylight."

He nodded toward the chief, taking his leave. The chief waved them on.

"You ever give any thought to being a drill sergeant?" Jonah asked her as he held the chief's office door open for Maggie. "Because you really should. I think you'd be perfect for the job."

"Think so?" she asked. When he nodded, she said cheerfully, "Then maybe I *will* give it some thought."

## Chapter 16

Dinner that evening was courtesy of an extremely grateful woman named Molly McClure who wanted to express her thanks to the team that had rescued her ten-year-old son, Nathan, who was buried alive beneath a pile of rubble earlier that week. Because the general store was receiving regular deliveries now, Molly was able to go all out with her preparations. She wouldn't allow any of the team or the volunteers to leave until they had all had at least two servings of her fried chicken, mashed potatoes, corn and something that was supposed to pass for a green salad.

It was a treat for the team to gather together, talking and sharing stories—doing something other than digging through debris.

Consequently, by the time Jonah and Maggie walked into his cabin, it was a great deal later than they had anticipated. They were both quite tired.

Even so, Maggie turned toward Jonah and smiled. "That was rather nice. I guess you're kind of used to this, aren't you?"

Exhausted, Jonah dropped his large frame onto the sofa. "You mean eating?" he asked. "Yeah, I try to do it at least once a day."

"No, wise guy," Maggie laughed at him. "I mean being regaled as a hero."

Jonah frowned in response, shaking his head. "I'm not a hero," he denied with feeling. "None of us are. We're just doing what we would want someone else to do if they were in the right place at the right time. Help," he concluded simply, eschewing any sort of fanfare beyond that.

But Maggie was not about to allow Jonah to brush off everything he'd done for the town and its residents so lightly.

"Yes, you are," she insisted. "It takes a certain kind of person to risk their lives to save others like that."

"You did it," Jonah pointed out. "I saw you," he reminded her. "You've been in the thick of things more than a few times since I got you out of that tree," he added with a grin.

Maggie sighed. The tree again. "You're not going to let me forget that, are you?"

The expression on his face told her that she was right.

"It still has some mileage in it," Jonah said glibly.

And then he grew a little more serious as he asked, "It doesn't really bother you, does it?"

"No," she admitted. "Not if it makes you smile like that." Although she really wished he didn't find so much amusement in his good deed.

"Know what else makes me smile?" Jonah asked, moving in closer to her.

Maggie looked up at him, a totally innocent expression on her face. "What?"

He didn't mind playing games when she turned out to be the prize. "You," he answered softly. The single word all but encompassed her.

"Oh?" Maggie questioned.

"Yeah, oh," Jonah echoed just as he leaned in to kiss her.

She felt herself melting even seconds before he made contact. He had the ability to really set her on fire with just one kiss.

"I thought you were tired," Maggie murmured against his lips.

His grin, beginning in his eyes, was positively wicked. "I guess I just got my second wind," Jonah said a beat before he took Maggie in his arms and kissed her again.

Maggie totally surrendered to the thrilling wave that came rushing over her.

She had every intention of making the most of this interlude while it lasted. She was more than aware that what was happening between the two of them had a limited life expectancy, because very soon, Jonah would be returning to Austin on a permanent basis.

That was where his job was, while her place, she had come to accept, was here.

With Bell marrying Donovan, there would probably be children on the horizon, and while she was undecided about having children of her own, "Aunt" Maggie was more than willing to pitch in and help her sister when Bell's children made their appearance.

With the immediate future, not to mention everything else, so up in the air right now, all she wanted to do was live in the moment.

And right now, the moment was delicious, she thought, her body heating as Jonah kissed her over and over again while they slowly made their way into the bedroom to make love.

Everything else was put on hold.


"I can't believe we're actually going to go back to that prison to see Elliott for a second time," Maggie said with a large sigh as she lay beside Jonah the following morning.

She had woken up before him and had been awake for a few minutes now. But she hadn't said anything or even attempted to get up until she had felt him stirring next to her.

Jonah slipped his arm around her now, bringing Maggie closer. "If you'd rather not, I can go alone," he told her, kissing the side of her head.

"Thanks, but I started this. I'm not about to bow out just because the man makes my skin crawl." She shivered just thinking about Corgan. "How could people not have caught onto him right from the beginning? For heaven sakes, the man almost *looks* the part of a crazy serial killer."

The moment the words her out of her mouth, other thoughts occurred to her. She had married into the family not knowing about its dark secret.

"For that matter, how did my ex's family manage to keep this all—the dead bodies, Elliott's conviction— quiet for so long?"

"You forget, money can buy almost anything, including silence," Jonah told her. "It also has a long reach," he added, "which was one of the reasons that I moved to Austin."

That caught her attention. Jonah hadn't really talked about what had made him leave Whisperwood before.

Maggie drew herself up on her elbow to look at him. "You wanted to get away from your family?" she asked, curious.

"No, just from their name," he told her. As he spoke, he played with the ends of her hair, tantalizing them both. "I wanted to be my own man, to know that whatever I accomplished, it wasn't because of the Colton name, but because of the effort I put into whatever career path I chose to follow." He smiled then, laughing at his own naïveté. "I never thought that my becoming part of the Cowboy Heroes would wind up bringing me right back to my hometown."

"Well, speaking for your hometown," she said, "I'm very glad that it did."

"Just speaking for the town?" he asked, arching a brow as he looked at her.

"And me," she added, knowing that was what he was going for. "That goes without saying."

The grin instantly reached his eyes. "Oh, say it," Jonah coaxed.

She ran the back of her hand along his cheek. "Okay. I'm very glad that you came back just in time," she told him.

"Otherwise," he said, enjoying himself, "you might still be up that tree."

"Don't push it, Colton," she warned. But there was a smile in her voice as she said it.

"Oh, but I like pushing you," he told her, stealing a quick kiss that threatened to blossom into something far more consuming.

But before she got too carried away—Jonah was quickly becoming her weakness—Maggie placed her hands against his chest to keep him from kissing her again. "We're going to wind up being late," she predicted.

"Corgan's not going anywhere. And we're not on the clock," he reminded her. "I think, all things considered, that he can wait an extra half hour or so for us, don't you think?"

Maggie gave up fighting Jonah as well as her own desires. "You're right," she agreed, happily surrendering to him—and herself.

Instead of the predicted half hour, it was closer to two hours later when they finally drove up to Randolph State Prison. Unlike the day before, this time the visitors' parking lot was fairly empty.

"See, I told you there was no reason to hurry," Jonah said to her. "Maybe if Corgan has to wait for a while, he'll be more inclined to talk so he doesn't wind up losing our attention." Jonah pulled up into the first row and parked his truck there. "Looks like we'll practically have the place to ourselves."

She looked around. There were about one quarter of the cars here today than were in the lot yesterday. "I'm not sure if I think that's a good thing or a scary one," she confessed.

"Nothing to be afraid of," Jonah reminded her. "I'm going to be right here with you." To illustrate his point, he took her hand.

Yes, he had a way of making her feel protected, but she couldn't get used to this, Maggie told herself. She was a realist. The town was already getting back on its feet, although it was rather wobbly. But the fact was that Whisperwood was starting to look better. Sure, there was still lots of work left to do, but reconstruction really wasn't part of Jonah's job. That meant that Jonah wasn't going to be around that much longer.

The thought left her cold.

As if to underscore that very point, Jonah let go of her hand. Without thinking, Maggie reached for it. He glanced in her direction and smiled. His fingers curled around hers.

Why did she find that so comforting? she asked herself. She'd always been able to stand on her own before, even when she was married to James. She could certainly do that again.

She just couldn't allow herself to grow dependent on Jonah, she thought fiercely.

But she continued to let him hold her hand as they made their way through the various gates and doors until they were finally in front of the prison guard who took their phones and their wallets from them, securing the items until they were ready to leave again.

"It's for your own safety," the guard recited mechanically. "You'll get your things back when you leave Randolph."

"That can't be soon enough for me," Maggie said to Jonah.

As before, a guard brought them to the large communal room. Jonah told a second guard the name of the prisoner they had come to see.

The second guard, a different man from the day before, frowned at them as if the request was personally putting him out.

"Take a seat," he all but snarled. "We'll bring the prisoner down to you."

As the guard left, Maggie looked around the communal room. There were only two other people there and they were already seated, each talking to the prisoner that they had come to visit.

"Looks like we have our pick of tables, too," she commented.

Jonah chose a table that was located in the very center of the room. It was visible from all angles.

"I guess this is a really slow day at Randolph," he said.

He waited for Maggie to sit down, then took the seat beside her.

Several minutes passed. Jonah looked at his watch. "I don't remember it taking them this long to bring Corgan down the last time."

"Maybe Elliott's stalling because he wants to make a grand entrance," Maggie guessed. "He's probably drawing this out for as long as he can because he knows that once he tells us who he thinks is responsible for Emmeline's murder, that's it. There's no more reason for us to come back again to talk to him. We'll have the information we need and we'll go from there—and he knows that."

Jonah looked at his watch again. "You're probably right," he replied, trying to contain his impatience.

But after another fifteen minutes had passed and Corgan still hadn't made an appearance, Jonah was on his feet, ready to find someone in authority to tell them what was going on.

"Something's wrong," he told Maggie. "Even if he was deliberately dragging his feet, Corgan should have been down here by now. Or at least the guard should have come back to tell us why Corgan was taking so long. Maybe Corgan isn't going to meet with you."

"Speak of the devil," Maggie said, tapping Jonah's shoulder. She pointed to the doorway. The guard who had gone to get the prisoner had returned.

"Looks like 'the devil's' alone," Jonah observed, annoyed. He crossed to the doorway with Maggie following closely behind him. "What's the matter?" Jonah asked the guard. "Why isn't Corgan with you?"

"If he's refusing to see us—" Maggie began, cutting in.

"He's refusing to see *everybody*," the guard informed her, a nasty edge to his voice.

Jonah was tired of playing games. "He can't do that," he protested.

"Yeah, he can," the guard contradicted, "if he's dead," he added.

"Dead?" Jonah repeated, stunned. The guard had clearly buried the headline. Deliberately?

"What do you mean, dead?" Maggie demanded, pushing herself in front of Jonah. "We just saw him yesterday," she declared.

"Well, yesterday, he was alive," the guard answered. "This morning it looks like he hung himself in his cell, using his bedsheet. And I'm the guy who found him," he added in disgust. "I had to get someone to help me cut him down. That's what took so long," he told Jonah, scowling as he obviously anticipated that was going to be Jonah's next question.

Jonah frowned. This didn't sound right to him. "Corgan hung himself just like that and nobody saw anything?" he asked the guard, annoyed by the vagueness of the whole situation. He was certain that someone was hiding something.

"What do you want from me?" the guard demanded. "This is prison, not a frat house. Nobody *ever* sees anything," the man snapped.

Though the guard's attitude annoyed him, what he'd just said really didn't surprise Jonah.

"I want to see the body," Jonah insisted.

"Sorry, buddy, you're gonna have to get your jollies somewhere else," the guard retorted.

"I am asking you officially," Jonah ground out between clenched teeth. "I'm Jonah Colton." For the first time in years, he stressed his last name. "And I'm part of Cowboy Heroes, the search and rescue team that just put in two weeks saving and digging Whisperwood out of the rubble that hurricane created. And this is Maggie Reeves," he said, gesturing toward Maggie. "That dead prisoner was her uncle." Jonah conveniently skipped over the part about Maggie no longer being married to Corgan's nephew. "Now, if you've got a drop of human decency in those veins of yours, you will take us to see the body," he told the guard.

The guard obviously didn't like being overridden. "How do I know you are who you say you are?" he challenged Jonah.

"You can check our IDs," Maggie told the guard. "They're being held by the guard up front." And then she changed directions. "Do you know if Elliott said anything to anyone before he died?"

"How the hell should I know that? I wasn't his nursemaid," the guard snapped. But then grudgingly, the guard relented. "Follow me. You can talk to the guard who helped me cut him down. It's the best I can do."

"This doesn't make any sense, you know," Maggie

insisted as they followed the guard. "Elliott wouldn't commit suicide," she insisted.

The guard turned around to look at her. "Why? Because he was so happy here?" the guard asked sarcastically.

"No, because when we spoke to him yesterday, he gave every indication that he intended to live a long, long time, enjoying all the attention that his 'handiwork' had garnered him. That's not a man who was planning on hanging himself in the morning."

"Look," the guard told them angrily, "all I know is that if you go talk to the other guard, he's not going to tell you anything different than I did."

Suddenly, as he brought them out into the corridor leading to the prison's interior, a shrill alarm sounded, calling for all visitors to immediately evacuate the prison.

# Chapter 17

"What's going on?" Jonah demanded

No one was answering him. Exasperated, he caught hold of Warren, the guard who was, until a moment ago, bringing them back to Corgan's cell.

There were guards armed with rifles rushing past them, while civilians there to visit prisoners were being evacuated, herded in the opposite direction, toward the exit.

Everything suddenly appeared to be in a state of chaos.

"There's a riot in Cell block C," Warren shouted, responding to a message that had just come through on his cell phone. "You have to go back the way you came," he told Jonah.

If he had come out here on his own, then Jonah

would have been perfectly willing to find his way out of the prison, no problem. But he wasn't alone. He had Maggie to think of and he wanted an armed escort to lead them out since he had no way to defend her or himself. He had surrendered his weapon along with his wallet and ID at the desk before they had passed through the last prison door.

"Look, man, you need to escort us out of here," Jonah insisted, raising his voice because the din coming from scrambling civilians and rioting prisoners was getting louder.

But the guard was just as adamant that they had to do as he said and part ways.

"Sorry, but we've all got our assigned duties in the event of a riot. Look," he said, leaning in so that his voice carried without the need to shout, "the prison is in the process of being locked down so my advice to you is to get the hell out of here. *Now*," he ordered. "Go that way," Warren said, pointing behind Jonah.

Annoyed, Jonah turned away from the guard and told Maggie, "We're on our own."

He found himself talking to no one.

"Maggie?" He repeated her name, looking around, but she was nowhere to be seen. A sense of growing panic instantly set in.

Where was she?

"Maggie!" he called out again. Receiving no answer, Jonah dashed after the guard and grabbed hold of Warren's wrist before the man was able to get away. "I can't find the woman who was just here with me."

Warren's ruddy complexion was even more flushed

than usual as he tried to pull free. The look on his face made it clear this wasn't his problem.

"Looks like she's smarter than you are and took off. If I were you, I'd do the same," he told Jonah, and made another attempt to pull free.

But Jonah just tightened his grip on the man's wide wrist. He wanted answers and he wanted the guard's help. "She wouldn't just take off like that," he all but growled at the guard. "Something must have happened to her."

Annoyance creased the man's low forehead. "Well, good luck with that. I've got a lockdown to deal with," he said again, trying to yank his wrist free of Jonah's grip.

"No," Jonah told the guard, measuring out each word evenly, "What you've got to deal with is helping me find her, you understand?"

"Look, jackass, I've—"

And then, whatever curse or choice words the guard had intended to utter never materialized. Instead, his small dark eyes widened in surprise as he pointed behind Jonah toward a scenario that was unfolding down the corridor.

When Jonah turned around, he saw that one of the inmates who had apparently managed to escape from Cell block C was holding a knife to Maggie's throat. He was dragging her back there with him.

"You do what I tell you to do, bitch, and maybe you'll live to see tomorrow." The escaped inmate, a man in his late thirties, was skinny and by the looks of him, he was obviously high on some kind of drug.

All it took was one look at the man's eyes to see that he was completely out of it.

Jonah's first instinct was to run toward Maggie and somehow wrestle the knife away from the inmate. But he knew that there was no way he could launch any kind of a frontal attack on the prisoner without also endangering Maggie, maybe even getting her killed.

"Do what he says, Maggie," Jonah called out to her. "Don't fight him."

"Listen to your boyfriend, honey, and you and me are gonna have us a real a good time," the inmate promised, leering as he dragged Maggie with him down the corridor. Within moments, both the inmate and Maggie disappeared from view.

The second he lost sight of Maggie, Jonah turned back to the guard. "Where does that corridor lead?" he demanded.

"That one? That goes back to Cell block C," the guard told him.

A chill washed over Jonah. He couldn't allow that to happen. "Do any other corridors intersect it before it gets to Cell block C?" he asked.

"I don't know. Maybe," Warren answered with a careless shrug.

Jonah resisted the temptation of shaking the information out of the guard. Instead, he kept his temper in check and said, "'Maybe' isn't good enough." When the guard didn't volunteer anything further, Jonah's face darkened.

"I'm not a violent man, but if anything happens to that woman, I'm going to devote my life to making sure you live to regret it. Now does any other corridor intersect with the one that inmate just dragged that woman down?" Jonah repeated.

The guard actually appeared to think for a second, fully aware that Jonah was tightening his grip on his wrist with each passing moment. "Yeah, yeah it does," he finally cried.

"Show me!" Jonah ordered, pushing the guard out in front of him.

"Look, you're just making things worse for yourself," Maggie said to the inmate who had the knife to her throat and was dragging her backward with him. She'd almost stumbled twice. "If you let me go now, things will go easier on you." It took everything she had for her to remain calm.

"What do you think I am, stupid or something?" the inmate shouted at her. "I let you go, I've got no leverage. Holding on to you is the only choice I've got. Besides, you have any idea how long it's been since I had my hands on a woman? Too damn long, that's how long," he yelled, taking out his frustration on her and becoming almost hysterical before he managed to calm himself down.

"Why don't you take that knife away from my throat?" Maggie suggested, keeping her voice friendly. "If you accidentally cut me, I'll be bleeding all over you and what fun would that be?"

"If I cut you, there won't be no 'accidentally' about it," the inmate promised her. "And you think I don't know that if I take the knife away from your throat, you'll take off?"

"I won't take off," Maggie told him, adding, "You have my word."

"Your word," the inmate mocked. "Like that means anything anymore." He continued dragging her with him, one arm held tightly around her waist, the other hand holding the knife to her throat. "Besides," he said, pausing just for a second to rub his face against her hair, "in case you haven't noticed, I'm getting off on this."

She could feel herself getting physically sick. She didn't have to use her imagination to know what the man had in mind for her.

"I'm not," she said, hoping that might make him view this Neanderthal action differently.

But instead, he just laughed at her, enjoying this unexpected turn of events. "Too bad. I am."

The inmate looked over his shoulder to make sure he was going in the right direction as he continued to drag her off with him.

The next part happened so fast, neither Maggie nor the inmate realized what was going on until it was almost over.

In the inmate's case, it wasn't until he felt a wire going over his head, around his throat and then tightening in one smoothly executed movement, deftly robbing him of the ability to get air into his lungs.

"Let her go, you brain-dead jackass," Jonah ordered. Furious, he tightened the wire even further. "Now!" he commanded.

Because he was suffocating, the inmate dropped
the knife he was holding to Maggie's throat. A gur-
gling sound was coming out of his mouth as he desperately tried to suck in some air.

The second the knife was away from Maggie's
throat, Jonah loosened the wire that he had gotten
around the inmate's throat, although he still held it in
place to show the man who was in control.

With Maggie free, Jonah stepped back and let the
guard take over restraining the inmate. Warren was
quick to jump in.

"You're not going anywhere," Warren snarled at
the inmate when the latter struggled, then sank down
to his knees. Warren yanked him back up to his feet.
"You're going back to your buddies. And then you're
all going to be getting what's coming to you," Warren informed the would-be escapee.

It was over as quickly as it had begun. All the prisoners were being herded back to their cell block, although they were all going to be kept separate from
one another until the responsible parties were singled out and properly dealt with. It was clear that
some heavy restrictions were going to have to be put
in force.

Jonah was oblivious to all this going on. His only
concern was Maggie.

"Are you all right?" he cried as Maggie all but col-
lapsed into his arms.

He held on to her for a long moment, incredibly relieved that he could. There had been one really scary

moment back there when he was afraid that this whole scenario was not going to end well for her.

Jonah upbraided himself for ever having brought her back here, but at the same time he knew it was futile to feel guilty about it. Maggie was stubborn. She would have come here on her own and if he hadn't been with her, who knows what might have happened?

"I'm fine," Maggie assured him in a somewhat-shaky voice.

But he wanted to see for himself, to check her over and make sure that the deranged inmate hadn't cut her or left any kind of a mark on her from that knife he'd been holding against her throat.

Because if he had, if the prisoner had left even the tiniest scratch on her, he was going to come back and make the man pay for that.

"I just want to make sure for myself," Jonah told her.

Satisfied that there wasn't so much as a scratch on her, he took Maggie back into his arms, embracing her as if he had separated from her for an entire eternity. It certainly felt that way to him.

"When I saw that lowlife holding that knife to your throat, I swear my heart froze. I just wanted to rip *his* heart out with my bare hands," Jonah told her.

Holding her to him, he kissed the top of Maggie's head several times over. He felt his own heart twisting as he relived the scene in his head. "I've never been so scared in my life, Maggie," he admitted quietly. "Scared that I was going to lose you."

"No such luck," she murmured against his chest, her breath warming him.

"Luck?" Jonah repeated, then held her away from him for a moment to get a better look at her face. "I wouldn't call losing you 'luck,' Maggie," he said, enfolding her in his arms again. "If anything ever happened to you, I really don't think that I could continue."

This time Maggie was the one who drew back to look up at his face, confused as she tried to process what Jonah was telling her.

"Just what are you saying, Jonah?" she asked, afraid to think what she was thinking.

Jonah paused for a moment then, drawing in a breath and pulling his thoughts together as best as he could. This was a new concept he was dealing with.

"I guess what I'm saying is that I love you," he told Maggie.

It was hard to know who was more surprised to hear him say that, Maggie or him. But once the words were out, he knew that they were true. He found himself smiling at her.

"Yup," he said, "I love you. And I don't ever, ever want to go through anything even close to that again."

Dazed by his revelation as well as by what had happened earlier, she nodded. "All right, then I guess I'll cross off prison riots from my list of preferred activities," she said with such a straight face, for a second she almost sound serious.

It took Jonah half a minute to realize that she was

kidding. He laughed then, the sound echoing with almost-tangible relief.

"That's just fine with me," he told her. And then he looked her over one final time "You're sure that you're okay?"

"Jonah Colton," Maggie said, threading her arms around his neck, "I have never been so okay in my whole life. Really."

"Then let's go home," he told her, putting his arm around Maggie's shoulders. "There's nothing we can do here now that Corgan's dead."

"His 'suicide' is still rather fishy to me," she told Jonah as they began to walk toward the front desk.

He had no intention of disagreeing with her. "I guess we can just add that to the list of things that need looking into," he told her.

Their escape from the prison grounds was delayed when Warren, the guard who had brought Jonah to the corridor that intersected with the one the escaped inmate had taken returned. He placed himself in front of the couple to momentarily prevent their exit.

Jonah instinctively positioned himself between the guard and Maggie just in case something else was about to happen.

"Hey, in all the excitement," the guard said, "I forgot to ask you if either one of you wanted to press charges against Waylon."

"Against who?" Jonah asked, not recognizing the name the guard used.

"Waylon Roberts," the guard said, "the guy who held a knife to your girl's throat."

"Absolutely," Jonah responded. "But can we come back tomorrow to do that?" He looked toward Maggie. She nodded her agreement. "I think we both just want to get out of here for now."

"Sure. I understand," the guard said, much friendlier now with the riot quelled than he had been just less than a half hour ago. "You want an escort out?" he offered.

Jonah looked at Maggie again and she nodded. "Sure, that would be good," he agreed for both of them. "Thanks."

The guard accompanied them not just through the first set of gates, but he also came with them when they picked up their personal possessions.

Warren seemed impressed when he saw Jonah's handgun. "That's a beauty." And then he asked, "You have everything you came with?"

"That, plus a whole lot of adrenaline I didn't even realize I had coursing through my veins," Maggie replied, speaking up.

"Yeah," the guard said as if he was accepting partial blame for that. "I'm really sorry you had to go through all that."

She appreciated the apology. "All that matters is that it ended well."

The guard stood and waved them on their way, which surprised them.

"That was pretty gracious of you," Jonah remarked as they left the man behind them, "considering that if someone at the prison hadn't dropped the ball, you would have never had a knife pressed against your throat." He took her hand as they left the building. Then, glancing at her face and seeing her expression, he had to ask, "What are you smiling about?"

"That guard, he called me your girl," Maggie answered.

"All right," Jonah responded, still waiting to hear why she was smiling like that.

Her eyes met his. "And you didn't correct him."

"No," he agreed. "I didn't. Because he was right—unless of course, you don't want to be," he interjected. Maybe she'd been offended by that, he thought. "I guess that is rather an adolescent term," Jonah admitted, watching her expression.

"And just what's wrong with using a term that adolescents use?" she asked. "All my best friends were adolescents once upon a time."

He put his arm around her shoulders and pulled her to him, laughing. "Funny you should say that. Mine were, too."

## Chapter 18

By the time Jonah had pulled his truck up in front of the cabin, he had put everything else out of his mind except for one all-consuming thing. He desperately wanted to make love with Maggie. After almost losing her in the prison riot, he had realized just how very precious she was to him.

If there was anything else even remotely on his mind, it was trying to come up with a way to re-arrange his life so that he could come back to Whisperwood on a permanent basis and live here. But he intended to tackle those logistics *after* Donovan and Bellamy's wedding had taken place.

Right now, all he wanted was to lose himself in Maggie. Everything else was a distant, *distant* second.

Looking back, Jonah was certain that if he hadn't

been so terribly preoccupied, he would have noticed that something was off even before he approached the front door.

Which he discovered was slightly ajar.

He turned toward Maggie, puzzled. "Did you leave the front door unlocked?" He didn't think it was like her, but he had to ask.

"No, and besides that, you were the last one who left the cabin," she reminded him. Maggie stared at the door. This didn't feel right. "And you always lock the door after you." She bit her lower lip. After the prison riot, they were both admittedly a little paranoid. "Maybe there's something wrong with the lock. It is old," she pointed out.

"Get behind me," Jonah ordered. "Maybe it's nothing, but there might be an animal in there. If there is, it's most likely foraging for food." If it *was* an animal, Jonah wanted to make sure that it didn't attack Maggie.

Maggie just thought that Jonah was focusing on an animal getting into the cabin to put her at ease. Had there been someone here?

She didn't hear any sounds of movement coming from inside. This *wasn't* an animal.

"You know any wild animals that 'almost' close the door behind them?" Maggie asked. She nodded at the door that they had found ajar.

Jonah shrugged. "First time for everything." His hand on the doorknob, he carefully turned it and then slowly pushed the door open.

The moment he looked inside, adrenaline blasted

through him like an exploding grenade. Why hadn't he seen this coming?

His grandmother's rocking chair had been moved and positioned so that it was just a foot away from the door. Sitting in the rocking chair was James Corgan, Maggie's ex-husband.

He was holding a large handgun, which was now aimed right at Maggie. "Sure took you a long time to get back from the state prison, Mags," James commented.

"What the hell are you doing in my cabin?" Jonah demanded.

"Waiting for you, obviously," James replied curtly. "Or rather, for my winsome ex-wife here." His eyes slowly traveled down the length of Maggie's body with the air of a man who felt that he still owned her. "I see you managed to make it out of the prison riot in one piece." He shook his head bemoaning the fact. "What a pity."

Maggie was instantly alert. "How do you know about the prison riot?" she demanded. Had her ex-husband orchestrated it?

James appeared to be bored by the question. "I'm a Corgan. My family practically owns this area. Nothing happens around here without me knowing it."

"The riot wasn't 'around here,'" Jonah informed the other man coldly. "It took place in Randolph State Prison. That's in Austin."

James's eyes darkened. "I *know* that. But since dear old crazy uncle Elliott has been in that prison for what amounts to decades now, I consider Randolph to be part of the family's sphere of interest, as well," James answered with the air of someone who felt he was entitled to everything and anything he wanted.

On his feet now, he continued to study his ex-wife like someone trying to find the answer to a riddle. "If you don't mind my asking, how did you manage to get away from that hulking drug addict? He was at least twice your size if not bigger."

Incensed, Jonah suddenly demanded, "Did you have anything to do with that?"

James's expression mocked him. "Do I look like the type to kiss and tell?" he smirked.

"You worthless piece of garbage," Jonah spit. He didn't know how yet, but he would bet anything that James was somehow behind that riot *and* behind that addict getting a knife so he could attack Maggie. "That addict held a knife to Maggie's throat," Jonah shouted angrily, taking a step closer to James.

The latter cocked his gun. "Too bad he didn't plunge it in up to the hilt. That was what he was supposed to do, not grandstand and draw the process out," James informed them, lamenting the inmate's failure. "Don't take another step, Boy Scout," he warned Jonah. "You might be good when it comes to digging through dirt, but you're not fast enough to outrun a bullet." His smile was positively chilling. "Although you're welcome to try," he taunted, aiming his gun at Jonah.

"Jonah, don't," Maggie warned, putting her hand on Jonah's arm to keep him back. "He's a trained shot. He likes to show off for his friends at the local firing range."

"I'd listen to her if I were you, Joe-naw," James said, deliberately drawing out Jonah's name and ridiculing him.

"What is it you want from us, James?" Maggie asked her ex-husband angrily. "Why are you in Jonah's cabin, playing these games?"

"No games, Mag-pie," James denied, taking a step closer to Maggie. "You were the one who liked to play games, remember?"

She looked at him as if he was crazy. "What are you talking about?" Maggie demanded. "What games?"

The cold-blooded smile vanished, replaced by a look of sheer hostility. "Then what would *you* call marrying me for my money?" he demanded.

"I didn't marry you for your money, James," Maggie denied passionately. There was hatred mingled with pity in her eyes. "I married you because I loved you. Until I didn't."

"You loved me," James mocked, his hand tightening on the handgun. "Is that why you took me for half my money?" he demanded.

Jonah watched the other man's every move, bracing himself to jump in and defend Maggie if the need arose.

Maggie's eyes were blazing. "Call it a consolation prize for putting up with all your womanizing," she retaliated. "And it wasn't half your money. I just took what I felt was due me," she told the man she had come to loathe. "I wanted to give the money to my parents to help get them out of debt, but they died before the terms of our divorce were even drawn up."

"So I was right. You were just a greedy whore," James accused.

Maggie held on to Jonah's arm again, restraining him. She had no doubt that he wouldn't think twice about beating the living daylights out of James, but she didn't want Jonah hurt and James was still holding on to his handgun, aiming it at them.

"I gave the money to Bell to buy our old house," she told her ex.

James's complexion turned a bright shade of red. "You used my money to buy your sister a house?" he shouted, livid.

"No," Maggie calmly corrected, her voice the complete opposite of her ex-husband's, "I used *my* money to buy my sister our old house."

Instead of screaming curses at her, James surprised them by laughing. It was the laughter of a man who was coming unhinged.

Regaining control over himself, he wiped away the tears that had rolled down his cheeks.

"Who would have ever thought that someone with such a gorgeous face and killer body could actually be able to think things through like that? Such a surprise," he told her, nodding to himself. And then he sobered. This time the hatred was back in his eyes. "Why did you have to leave me?" he asked, fury mingled with self-pity vibrating in his voice.

"Why did you have to cheat?" Maggie countered, refusing to be intimidated.

"Because I'm a man," James shouted into her face. "It's the way of the world. All men cheat."

Instead of Maggie, it was Jonah who spoke up. "No, they don't," he told James, looking at the man as if doing so turned his stomach and made him sick. "Not unless they're insecure."

Rage entered James's face. "What the hell do you know?" he challenged.

"I know a good thing when I see one," Jonah answered, still exceedingly calm as he glanced toward Maggie. "And I know how not to do something stupid to screw things up and lose her."

"So is that it?" James demanded, all but spitting out the question as he asked it. He turned toward Maggie. "He's your new boy toy?"

Maggie raised her chin proudly, a woman who wasn't about to be cowed. "He's not anybody's toy, James. Jonah just opened my eyes and made me realize that not every man is a pig like you."

James seemed to go blind with rage, clutching his handgun. "I'd watch my mouth if I were you, Magpie. You won't be able to kiss your cowboy hero if I shoot it off," he warned.

Jonah curled his fingers into his hands, fighting the very strong urge to strangle Maggie's ex. "Don't threaten her," he warned.

"You're right," James agreed, underscoring his words with almost a maniacal laugh. "Besides, this dumb blonde can't be scared off with just threats anyway."

Maggie's eyes widened as everything fell into place. "That was you," she cried. "You're the one who's been sending me those awful anonymous email threats, aren't you?"

"And you're the one who's too dumb to pay attention to them," James screamed at her in sheer frustration.

Jonah moved in closer, intent on shielding Maggie with his own body. "Why did you send her those texts?" he asked.

"Why?" James echoed, stunned that the other man had to even ask. "Because if she wasn't going to stay married to me, I didn't want her digging into my family, not even into my loony old uncle Elliott for any reason. She doesn't get to do that."

"So you threatened her instead?" Jonah asked, stunned that anyone would think of that as a reasonable course of action.

"Hey, if she's not willing to be on my arm and act like my eye candy, then I've got nothing to lose," James responded. "Too bad that idiot addict botched the job. Just shows, if you want something done right, you have to do it yourself," he sighed, raising his gun and taking aim.

But Jonah moved farther in front of Maggie. He had to stall for time. "But why did you have your uncle killed?" Jonah asked.

James looked at him as if he was insane. "I didn't, not that it's any business of yours. As far as I know, that crazy old loon did away with himself. Well, good riddance. But I had nothing to do with that."

Jonah didn't believe him. "And I suppose you're also going to deny knowing anything about the person who killed Emmeline Thompson."

Fury washed over James's face again. Being accused of doing things that he had had no part in didn't sit well with him.

"How would I know anything about a woman who was killed almost before I was born?" James demanded. His eyes washed over the two people in the room with him. There was nothing but pure hatred in his eyes. "You two are really made for each other, you know that?" he declared maliciously.

James's eyes narrowed as he pointed his gun at first one, then the other, wanting to make them sweat. It infuriated him that neither flinched. "And that's why it seems like some kind of poetic karma that you're going to die together."

"You don't want him, you want me," Maggie cried, shifting quickly so that her body was blocking Jonah's instead of the other way around. "You don't have any reason to hurt Jonah."

"Sure I do," James said mockingly. "I don't like his face. And neither will you," he predicted. "When I'm finished."

Maggie stared at the man who had once been her husband, horrified. How could she have ever been in love with this man, even for a moment? He was a disgusting, depraved, poor excuse of a man. Even his good looks were beginning to wane, a casualty of James's unbridled love for all manner of alcohol, it didn't matter what kind.

But even if he was still as good-looking as the day she had met him, it was his black soul that had pushed her away and made her not want to have anything to do with him.

"Leave him alone," she cried when she saw James begin to take careful aim at Jonah. "You want me? You have me," she told her ex. "But on the condition that you leave Jonah alone."

"Oh, how very touching," James hooted, turning his attention toward Maggie. "Maybe I don't want you anymore," he told her, the look on his face growing downright menacing and ugly as he shifted his gun to point straight at Maggie. "You're tainted goods now."

It was now or never, Jonah thought. And since he couldn't think of anything to distract James and get him to leave Maggie alone, he knew he had to do something drastic, something James wasn't expecting before the other man could follow through on his overwhelming, all-consuming hatred.

"Get out of the way, Maggie!" Jonah yelled. Ducking his head down, he dived straight for James, throwing the other man off and knocking him to the floor.

The handgun discharged, sending two shots into the ceiling.

"You son of a bitch!" James cried, scrambling to recover both his balance and his weapon.

But Jonah was faster and he managed to pull out the gun he had kept tucked in the back of his belt since before he had left his truck. A gut feeling had been responsible for his taking his gun along, and now he was really glad that he had followed that instinct. He had just been waiting for the right opportunity to catch the other man unaware.

"Don't move!" he warned James, pointing the handgun at him.

The expression in the other man's eyes was wild. "What the hell do I have to lose?" James cried, trying to reach for his own gun.

Jonah discharged his weapon, but it was only to shoot the butt of the other gun out of James's reach.

"Don't do it," Jonah warned again. "Leave the weapon where it is."

"Sorry, can't do that," James responded, once again trying to go for his gun only to have Jonah shoot it away, out of his reach for a second time.

James looked at Maggie. The look on her face was one of pity. That only incensed her ex-husband further. He was about to lunge for his handgun one last time when the sound of approaching sirens pierced the otherwise-still air.

A look of frustrated panic came over James's face.

Even Maggie was surprised.

"How would they know to come here?" she asked Jonah. It seemed like a highly unlikely coincidence and she had stopped believing in coincidences a long time ago.

With his free hand, his eyes never leaving James, Jonah reached into his pocket. "Maybe because I dialed Thompson when I saw that the cabin door was opened. He's been listening to you rave the entire time," he told James.

With a guttural shriek, James was about to launch himself at Jonah. But before that could happen, the chief and two of his men burst into the cabin thanks to the unlocked door. Their guns were drawn and all three guns were pointed at James.

James swung around toward his handgun, his intentions obvious.

"I wouldn't do that if I were you, son," Thompson warned James. "You don't want people knowing that the last thing you ever did on this earth was something incredibly stupid."

James was breathing hard like the whipped animal he had become. "I've got nothing to lose," he growled.

"You've your life and where I come from, that's still plenty big. Step away from the gun. Your daddy wouldn't want you to die this way."

At the mention of his late father, James looked subdued. Still angry, he reluctantly stepped back from his weapon on the floor.

"You win this time," he said grudgingly to Maggie.

But Jonah was the one who answered him. "You're wrong. She's won for all time," he informed Maggie's former husband. Then, looking at Thompson, he said, "Sorry, Chief." Before the chief could ask him what he was sorry for, Jonah hauled off and punched James square in the face, sending the other man flat on his back. "That's for pointing a gun at Maggie," he told the crumpled heap on the floor. And then he turned toward Thompson. "You can arrest me now, Chief."

"For what?" Thompson asked. "I didn't see anything. Get this piece of garbage back to jail, boys," he ordered. "Looks like he's got more of his uncle in him than his daddy," the chief added. He smiled when he saw Maggie sink against Jonah. "You can come in tomorrow to press charges," he said. "We'll see ourselves out. Be sure to lock the door." He glanced toward the man his officers were taking out between them. "Never know what can come slithering in when you least expect it."

With that, Thompson closed the door behind him.

# Chapter 19

"You know, I was really starting to doubt that this day would ever get here," Maggie confided to her older sister.

She and Bellamy were looking themselves over in the full-length mirror one last time. The wedding ceremony was only minutes away from beginning.

Maggie found that she was *really* nervous for Bellamy. It surprised her that the latter looked like calmness personified.

"I know what you mean, what with first the hurricane, then the flood, it felt as if we were never going to find an island of time to have this ceremony in front of our family and friends," Bellamy agreed, adjusting her headpiece. It seemed a little lopsided to her.

Maggie was about to add the prison riot and James showing up at Jonah's cabin with his gun to that list, but then decided that, at least for now, she would keep those things to herself. There was no point in possibly ruining Bell's day with talk of what *might* have happened if things had gone badly. What counted was that they *hadn't* happened.

And more importantly, what mattered was that they were all finally gathered here to see her sister and Jonah's brother exchange their vows in front of all their loved ones.

Maggie's eyes met her sister's in the full-length mirror that had had been brought into this small room just for this occasion.

"I really wish that Mom and Dad had lived to see this," Maggie told her.

Bellamy's eyes became misty. "Yes, me, too," she agreed quietly.

Maggie squeezed her sister's hand, silently offering support.

"They've got a front row seat in heaven, watching over you. And if you ask me, I think they're going to be crazy about their new son-in-law," she confided.

Bellamy smiled. "I think so, too. All I know is that I'm glad you're here."

"And Donovan," Maggie reminded her, tongue in cheek. "Don't forget Donovan."

"No," Bellamy said with a wistful, faraway tone, "I'm certainly not about to forget Donovan," she told her sister with a laugh.

"Hey, how's it going in here?" Rae Lemmon

asked, sticking her head into the room. Her expression looked resigned as she took a look at Maggie. "Well, maybe I should drop out of the wedding party."

"Wait, what?" Bellamy cried. "Why?" Her calm exterior instantly threatened to crumble. At this point, she couldn't bear the idea of facing even a thimbleful of stress, much less anything else. She just wasn't up to it.

"Well, we're supposed to be co–maids of honor and I don't look anywhere near as good as Miss Beauty Contest Winner over there," Rae said, jerking a thumb in Maggie's direction. "Compared to Maggie, I look like one of Cinderella's ugly stepsisters," Rae complained. "Or a least the plain one."

"You think that's something—how would you like to have grown up with her? People would take one look at Maggie and then they would look at me again and ask, 'What happened to you? Were you adopted?'"

Having been a beauty contest winner had its downside, but Maggie had never become vain about those so-called "crowns" she had won. She had never been that shallow.

"Stop it, both of you," she ordered. "Beauty is in the eyes of the beholder and as far as I'm concerned, both of you are gorgeous. Besides, I hate to be the one to tell you this, Rae, but nobody's going to be looking at either of us. Every eye in the place is going to be looking at the bride here." Maggie gestured toward Bellamy. "Thinking how beautiful she looks."

"Terrific, now you've finally made me nervous," Bellamy complained.

Maggie gave Bellamy a quick hug, taking care not to wrinkle her sister's wedding gown. "There's nothing to be nervous about, Bell. You are going to be marrying the love of your life. Just remember to say 'I do' when the Reverend feeds you the line and everything will be just great."

Overwhelmed for a moment, Maggie hugged Bellamy again, this time harder. "You look just beautiful, Bell," she whispered. "Really." Releasing her sister, Maggie stepped back and looked at Rae. "Is everybody ready?"

Rae nodded. "Quick," she urged, "let's do this before anything else happens."

Maggie laughed. "Amen to that," she told her sister's best friend. Turning toward Bellamy, she said, "C'mon, big sister." Maggie gathered up her sister's long train. "Let's get you married."

Taking a deep breath, Bellamy smoothed down the sides of her gown and nodded.

Maggie cocked her head, listening. The beginning strains of The Wedding March could be heard echoing through the air.

"And there's the music, right on cue," Maggie commented.

Rae opened the door and all three of them filed out of the small back room.

"I can't believe she's really married," Maggie said again. She had lost count of how many times she had voiced that thought.

They were all at the reception. Dinner had been

served and eaten, although some of the slow eaters were still at it.

Despite everything the town had just gone through, somehow they had managed to put together a band to play at Bellamy and Donovan's reception. Hearing the music somehow made everything seem brighter and hopeful.

Taking advantage of having a live band there, Maggie had gone up to Jonah and asked him to dance. She was actually prepared to have to drag him onto the small dance floor, but to her surprise, Jonah had gone along with her willingly.

The first dance was a relatively fast number, but the next one was slow. It felt perfect to have his arms around her.

"I don't think either one of them quite believe it, either," Jonah said, nodding toward the bride and groom, who were also on the floor, dancing.

"I guess it's going to take some time to sink in," Maggie commented. And then she turned her attention back to her partner. He had really surprised her. "You dance well."

Jonah laughed at the stunned expression on her face. "You were expecting me to trip over my own feet, weren't you?"

"Well, not exactly that," Maggie quickly corrected. "But, well, you're a Cowboy Hero, you spend all your time looking for lost people and rescuing them," she explained. "That doesn't exactly leave much time over for any dancing."

"Sure it does," he told her with a straight face.

"My team and I do a little victory dance every time we find someone."

"You don't have to make fun of me," she told him, although she had to admit that probably from his point of view, she did have it coming.

"Oh, but it's so much fun to do that," Jonah confessed—just before he stole a quick kiss.

The slow song they were dancing to ended, but another one quickly started, taking its place. Because it felt so utterly right to be holding her like this, Jonah just continued dancing with Maggie.

"You know I'm just kidding, right?" he asked her. The last thing he wanted was to hurt Maggie's feelings.

She lifted her shoulders in a quick, fleeting shrug. "Everyone's got to have a hobby, I guess."

That made him think. "Well, if we're going to be talking about hobbies, I guess this is the right time to tell you that I've been thinking about taking up a new one," he told her.

Listening, she wasn't sure just where he was going with this. "Oh?"

"Yes." Now that he had gotten started, he was determined to push through this, even though he felt as if his gut was tying itself up in knots. "I've been thinking about this for a long time now and unless you have any objections—"

"Me?" Maggie cut in, confused. "Why would I have any objections to your new hobby?" she asked.

He looked down into her face. "Because my new hobby is you."

Maggie stopped dancing. "Excuse me?"

"I said my new hobby is yo—"

She shook her head, waving away the rest of his sentence. "I heard what you said, but how can I be your new hobby?"

"Because," he continued, smiling into her face, his courage growing, "I intend to learn every little thing there is to know about you." he told her.

He still wasn't being clear, Maggie thought. "Why would you want to do that?"

"Because," he told her, playing with a stray lock that had worked its way out of her carefully arranged hairstyle, "I think that a husband *should* know everything about his wife."

To say that she was stunned was a colossal understatement.

"Wait, hold it," Maggie cried.

Grabbing his hand she led him away from the small area that had been designated for dancing and drew him over to the far side of the rec center, away from all the other wedding guests.

Only when they had finally gotten clear of everyone did Maggie let go of his hand and turn around to face him. "Did you just miss a step? Because I know that I did."

His expression never changed. "I thought we were dancing very well."

"I'm not talking about dancing together," she insisted, feeling disoriented, not to mention more than a little confused.

"But I am," Jonah told her, then added very seriously, "I am talking about dancing together for the rest of our lives."

"Wait," Maggie ordered, putting her hand on his chest as if to underscore the instruction she had just managed to utter. Her pulse was racing so fast, she was certain he could detect it. "Back up here."

Maggie felt as if she was having a total out-of-body experience, which, considering everything else she had been through recently, didn't really surprise her as much as it should have.

But maybe she was just reading too much into this. Maybe there was another meaning entirely to what Jonah was saying to her, but if there was, for the life of her, she couldn't find it.

"Are you asking me to marry you?" she questioned Jonah very slowly, afraid that she had gotten her signals crossed somehow. She watched his face to see if he would suddenly start to laugh.

But he didn't.

There it was, he thought. There was the question. The answer could either make him or break him entirely, not to mention that the wrong answer would suck up his soul.

But now that it was out on the table between them like this, there was no running from it, no stalling to buy more time so that when Maggie finally gave him her answer, it was the one that he was hoping to hear.

"Well, Colton?" she pressed, waiting for him to answer her. "Are you?"

"In my own halting, totally mixed-up way, yes,"

he answered. "But in my defense, I've never done this before."

"You've never asked a woman to marry you before?" Maggie asked incredulously.

How could someone as handsome as Jonah have gotten to this stage of his life without asking someone to marry him? It didn't seem possible—unless he wanted to be a bachelor forever.

"No," he admitted, "I never have. And before you ask me why, it's because I never found anyone I *wanted* to ask, never found anyone I wanted to spend the rest of my life with—until now," he said, cupping her cheek for a moment. His eyes all but made love to her as he looked deeply into hers.

Maggie stared at him, afraid to believe what she was hearing. "You mean me?" she asked haltingly.

"Of course I mean you. Unless," Jonah qualified as it occurred to him that maybe she hadn't already said yes because she didn't want to, "the reason you haven't said yes is because you're trying to find a way to turn me down."

"After that prison riot and then coming home to find yourself looking down the barrel of my ex-husband's gun, I'm surprised you even want to talk to me, much less marry me," she told him.

"Oh, trust me, I want to do much more than that to you," he told her. She still hadn't said what he was waiting to hear. Taking a deep breath, Jonah resigned himself to the disappointment that was coming. "But if you'd rather I just walked away and left you alone, I will."

Maggie could only stare at him as she shook her head. "Amazing."

Jonah didn't understand what she was saying. "What is?"

"That a man like you who is so incredibly clever that you can pick up a trace of a clue at fifty paces can be so unbelievably thickheaded when it comes to seeing what is blatantly right in front of you," she marveled.

It just made her love Jonah that much more, she thought.

"And what is it that's right in front of me?" he asked Maggie, afraid that he was going to get it all wrong after all.

She turned her face up to his. "Me, Jonah, Me. I love you, you big dummy."

Relieved beyond belief, Jonah smiled into her eyes as he wrapped his arms around her waist. In the background, there was another song beginning to play, but he remained where he was, in the recesses of the rec center, content to be there with his girl in his arms.

"Good answer," he told her just before lowering his mouth to hers.

Lord, but he could get lost in that kiss of hers, Jonah thought. But this wasn't the time or the place to let that happen. He owed it to his brother to stay here for at least a large part of the reception even though every fiber of his being was begging him to just sweep Maggie up in his arms and go home with her. To make love with her until there was nothing left of either one of them but desire.

He was torn between duty and desire.

Maggie drew her lips back, afraid that with any more provocation, she was going to forget where she was and allow her crumbling barriers to just fall to the ground without an ounce of care.

But there were things that had to be settled. She couldn't just let all this happen blindly.

"Where are we going to live?" she asked him. She felt his arms tightening around her.

"Here." And then he explained why he'd changed his mind. "Your sister's here. My family's here. It only makes sense to put roots down here."

She wasn't going to let herself rejoice until she was absolutely sure he knew what he was doing—and why. "But what about your job in Austin?"

"After that hurricane and that flood, my organization is going to need an outpost here. There's no reason why I can't get transferred to Whisperwood," he told her.

"And what about making your name apart from the Colton name?" she asked. He had been pretty adamant about that.

Jonah shrugged as if that no longer mattered. "I did that. There's no point in proving myself over and over again. You have any more details to get in the way?" he asked her.

Her eyes crinkled at the corners as she smiled. "None that I can think of."

"Good. Then it's settled," he declared. "Except for just one thing," he reminded her.

"Oh?" She looked at him, a little confused. "What's that?"

"You haven't given me an answer."

"Maybe because you haven't actually come out and asked me that question," she countered.

"All right, let's do this the right way." Before she could ask him what the right way was, Jonah dropped down to one knee, took her hand and said, "Magnolia Reeves, will you marry me?"

"Yes, but if you ever call me Magnolia again," she warned him with feeling, "the wedding is off."

He rose to his feet, still holding her hand. "Duly noted," he said, pulling her back into his arms.

It was the last thing he said for a while. He had been raised right and knew it wasn't polite to talk when his lips were otherwise occupied.

# *Epilogue*

"I guess you must feel really relieved to finally be able to give your sister a proper burial, Chief," Mitch Cameron, one of Thompson's longtime police officers said. Cameron had come by to check with his superior before he called it a day and left the police station.

"Not as relieved as you might think, Cameron," Thompson answered. He'd been going through old paper files for the better part of the day. "Whoever killed my baby sister is still out there. The bastard needs to be made to pay for his crime."

Trying to comfort the chief, Cameron said, "You never know—maybe the guy's dead. That's always a possibility," he added hopefully.

But the chief shook his head. "My gut tells me

he's still out there, Cameron. And," he added grimly, "I don't think that Emmeline was his only victim."

Cameron looked at the stack of files on the chief's desk. "Is that why you've been going through all those old missing persons case files?"

"Missing *women* case files," Thompson corrected. That same hunch that told him the killer was still out there also told him that the killer had a type.

"Maybe the way he buried your sister, mummifying her body and burying her deep in the earth, shows that he regretted what he did," Cameron suggested, watching the chief's face for a reaction.

"Or maybe he just didn't want her body found by a cadaver dog," the chief countered.

Cameron laughed dryly. There was no humor in his laugh. "You sure aren't giving this guy any points, are you?"

"No, I'm not," Thompson all but growled at his officer. "You have anything else you want to say?" he asked, indicating that if he didn't, then Cameron should leave.

Cameron lingered by the door. "Just that I'm sorry about your sister, Chief."

Thompson sighed. He was letting all this get to him and he knew that an emotional crime investigator was a sloppy crime investigator, one who was liable to miss minute clues.

"Yeah, me, too," the chief answered, his tone losing some of its anger. "Good night, Cameron."

"Good night, sir," Cameron answered, walking out of the police station. He eased the door quietly closed behind him.

Cameron hadn't been gone for more than two minutes before the phone on Thompson's desk rang. He put a pencil—his use of pencils had been a running joke at the station for a while now—into the file he was reviewing to mark his place.

He picked up the receiver on the third ring and cradled it between his shoulder and his ear. "Thompson," he announced.

"Chief?"

Thompson recognized the voice as belonging to another one of his officers, Michael Juarez. Juarez had been part of the police force for only a year and a half. He had pulled the night shift. Everyone knew that usually meant that it was a good time to take cat-naps and get paid for them.

Thompson did his best not to lose his temper. "What is it, Juarez?"

"I think you're going to want to come down here, Chief. I found another dead body. It's wrapped up the same way that your sister was."

The young officer sounded scared, Thompson thought. He was already on his feet. "I'll be right there."

His gut instincts were right.

For once, Thompson really wished that he was wrong. But it looked like this case was far from over.

Maybe he'd finally get those answers about Emmeline's murder.

\* \* \* \* \*

*Don't miss the next story in this exciting series:*
Colton 911: Baby's Bodyguard
*by Lisa Childs.*
*For a short excerpt, turn the page...*

# Chapter 1

Her eyes wide and glazed with fear and death, she stared up at him—as if appealing to him for help. She wasn't the only one.

"Come on, Forrest," his brother Donovan implored. "Whisperwood PD needs your expertise."

Forrest gestured at the body lying amid the piles of dirt where Lone Star Pharma had intended to expand their parking lot. The drug company had had to put their plans on hold once the asphalt crew had dug up the body. "This isn't a cold case."

She couldn't have been buried that long; the body had barely begun decomp. Not that he was that close to the scene, which the techs were still processing. He'd wanted to stay back—out of the way. But his brothers had urged him closer.

"This isn't the only body that turned up recently," Jonah, the oldest of his brothers, chimed into the conversation. He and Donovan had picked up Forrest from their parents' ranch and brought him out here. Now he understood why. They were trying to get him involved in the investigation.

They stared at him now. And even though Donovan wasn't biologically their brother, he looked more like Jonah than any of his biological brothers. They were both dark haired and dark eyed whereas Forrest's hair was lighter brown and longer than their buzz cuts, and his eyes were hazel.

"There have been too many casualties," Forrest agreed.

A dozen people had lost their lives due to the flooding and wind damage Hurricane Brooke had wreaked on Whisperwood, Texas. Despite being early in the season, it had been deadly.

"That's why we're here—to help out because of the natural disaster," he reminded his brothers. They were part of the Cowboy Heroes, a horseback rescue organization formed years ago by ranchers and EMTs. Forrest had volunteered to help the Heroes' search and recovering efforts, not the police department. "And this isn't a natural disaster."

Though this person might have been one of the people reported missing since the hurricane, the storm hadn't caused her death. From what Forrest could see in the lights that the Whisperwood PD forensics unit had set up to illuminate the crime scene, the young woman had bruising around her neck and on her arms and legs. She hadn't drowned or been struck by a fallen tree.

She'd probably been strangled and maybe worse…

A chill raced down his spine despite the warmth of the August night. And this had happened recently.

"This is murder," Jonah said. He must have noticed what Forrest had. "Just like the body that Maggie and I found last month." He shuddered now. "And that one definitely falls within your area of expertise."

Forrest shook his head. "Not anymore."

A shooting had forced his early retirement from the Austin Police Department's cold case unit. That shooting, and the pins that held together the shattered bones in his leg, were why he'd had to retire with disability and why, as a volunteer with the Cowboy Heroes, he was consigned to a desk, operating the telephones. He took the calls about what people were missing—loved ones and livestock. But he'd rather be out in the field with his brothers actually searching for those missing people and animals. Hell, he'd rather be back on the job. And they knew him so damn well that they all knew that.

Jonah lowered his voice to a gruff whisper and murmured, "Not because you don't want to."

Sure, he would love to go back to the job, but there was no way in hell that he could pass a physical now. Not with his leg.

As if he'd read his mind, Jonah continued, "But you can now. The chief will give you a special dispensation to help out as an interim detective."

The special dispensation pricked his pride, and

he clenched his jaw. "I don't need you all doing me any favors."

"You'd be doing me the favor," Donovan said. "I was just about to leave on my honeymoon when this call came in to the department." Donovan only helped out part-time with the Cowboy Heroes; he was a full-time K9 cop with Whisperwood PD.

"It's a mini honeymoon," Forrest reminded him. "You're not going to be gone long."

"But even when we get back, I'm going to be distracted," Donovan claimed. "Bellamy's pregnant."

Jonah chortled and slapped their brother's back. "That's great! That's wonderful news."

And with everything that had happened since the hurricane, good news was more than welcome.

"Congratulations," Forrest said, and he reached out and squeezed his brother's shoulder. Donovan and Bellamy so deserved their happiness. They'd been through so much recently.

"Thanks," Donovan said with a big grin. But then he glanced down at the body and shook his head. "She deserves someone's full attention, and the police department and the chief are just stretched too damn thin right now dealing with the aftermath of the hurricane."

And the other dead body…

The chief's sister. Had someone else really murdered her? Or was serial killer Elliot Corgan messing with everyone from beyond his grave?

Forrest wouldn't put it past the sadistic son of a bitch. When he'd been on the job, he'd dealt with quite a few serial killers. They got nearly as much enjoyment playing mind games with law enforcement as they did killing.

He glanced down at the dead girl. At least one thing was for certain; Elliot hadn't killed her. He wouldn't have been able to manage that from beyond the grave. Unless...

"You're already on the case," Jonah said with a slight smile. "I can see your wheels turning."

Forrest glared at his big brother, but he didn't deny it. Too many thoughts flitted through his mind. Was she one of the people presumed missing because of Hurricane Brooke? Had someone taken advantage of the storm to murder her, thinking that law enforcement would assume she'd been lost in the flooding that had followed the storm?

Chief Thompson had been moving around the crime scene talking to the techs and officers guarding the perimeter. Ignoring the reporters who shouted questions at him from the other side of the police tape, Whisperwood PD's top cop walked toward Forrest and his brothers. Thompson had been doing this job a long time, and his experience showed in the lines in his face and the way his shoulders sagged when he looked down at the body. He shook his head and sighed, and his Stetson slipped lower over his face.

Forrest had realized some years into his career that it would never get any easier to see someone dead, especially *murdered*, and the chief just proved that to him. He let his own hat slide down to shield his face.

Thompson turned away from the body to focus on Forrest now, his blue eyes sharp with intelligence and determination. "So you going to do it? You going to take the job?"

His brothers stared at him, nodding and smiling to encourage his acceptance. They probably figured this would be good for him, would get him back doing the job he loved. But when he'd been shot, the job wasn't the only thing he'd lost that he loved.

That experience had taught him never to risk his heart again. So the job was all he had—even if it was just a short-term assignment.

He nodded. "Yes, I'll take it."

Not for his sake, though, like his brothers obviously wanted. But for hers.

He stared down at the dead woman. To make sure she got the justice she deserved and that the killer would not hurt anyone else.

"He's so cute," Bellamy cooed as she cradled the baby against her chest and kissed the top of his head. He'd been born with a full head of soft brown hair— the same chocolatey color as his mama's. He also had her big brown eyes.

Rae's heart swelled with maternal pride. "Yes, he is," she said just as a yawn slipped out. He'd also been keeping her up nights with a bout of colic, and Bellamy's bed was so comfy Rae was tempted to take a nap right there amid the pile of clothes and the suitcase.

"Hey, you need to finish packing," Maggie told her sister as she pried the baby from Bellamy's arms. "You're supposed to be leaving for your honeymoon."

"I will," Bellamy said. "As soon as Donovan gets back from the crime scene."

Rae shuddered. "So another body's been found?" Twelve people had died in the hurricane, but she'd thought all the missing had been accounted for—thanks to the Cowboy Heroes recovery and rescue efforts.

Maggie had been one of the missing. Fortunately, she had been found alive. Jonah Colton hadn't just rescued her, though. He'd also fallen in love with the former beauty queen. A pang of wistfulness tugged at Rae's heart—not that she wanted anyone falling in love with her.

She was too busy with her two-month-old son and her law school classes and her new job as a paralegal to fit a man into her life right now. Or ever…

Connor was the only man for her. She smiled as he clutched his fingers around a lock of Maggie's pretty blond hair. Like every other male in Whisperwood, he was drawn to the former beauty queen.

Rae might have been jealous if Maggie wasn't as beautiful inside as she was on the outside. She twisted her pretty features into comical faces as she cooed at the fascinated baby. Then she glanced up at Rae and a frown pulled down the corners of her mouth. "From what the chief told Jonah, it sounds like the death had nothing to do with the hurricane."

Rae gasped. "Was it…like the body you and Jonah found?"

Maggie shuddered. "I hope not."

That body had been mummified. Rae hadn't seen

it, but just the thought of it had given her nightmares. She couldn't imagine what Maggie had gone through because of that and the threats to her life.

All the crime in Whisperwood was what had compelled Rae to take the LSAT to try to get into law school. Nobody had probably been as surprised as she was that she'd done so well that she had her pick of schools. Of course, she'd chosen to stay in Whisperwood with her friends. With her mom gone, they were the only family she had now—except for Connor. She'd already been pregnant with him when she'd taken the exam.

Bellamy nipped her teeth into her bottom lip. "Maybe Donovan and I shouldn't go away right now."

"No!" Rae and Maggie both shouted.

Connor, startled, began to cry. Rae jumped up from the bed and took him from Maggie. Holding him close, she smoothed her hand down his back and murmured, "It's okay, sweetheart. You're okay."

He settled down with a hiccuping sob. Then the tension drained from his tiny body and he began to drift off to sleep like Rae had longed to.

"You're so good with him," Maggie said with a smile.

"You are," Bellamy agreed. She looked more like Rae, with dark hair and eyes, and they'd known each other for so long, they were almost more like sisters than friends. "You're amazing. I can't believe how much you're doing all on your own."

Rae smiled with pleasure and pride. But then she reminded her friend, "You've done the same."

Maggie's mouth pulled down into another frown, and regret struck a pang in Rae's heart. She hadn't meant to cause any issues between the sisters. They'd already had too many.

"I was never alone," Bellamy said. "I had you, Rae." She turned toward Maggie and smiled at her sister. "And you... I just didn't realize what all you were doing for me."

"Rae's right," Maggie said. "You did all the heavy lifting on your own." Taking care of their ailing parents. "You deserve this honeymoon. You deserve every happiness. Don't let Donovan back out of going."

Bellamy smiled. "Not a chance. He's determined to go. He and Jonah are going to work on convincing Forrest to step in and take over the murder investigations."

Maggie nodded. "Oh, that's what big brother is up to." She'd fallen for the oldest of the Colton brothers. "He said he was going to pick up Forrest."

Another little pang struck Rae's heart at the mention of that particular Colton brother. It was probably just regret again. She shouldn't have asked him to dance at Bellamy and Donovan's wedding. But as one of the co—maids of honor, she'd wanted to make sure every guest enjoyed himself. That was the only reason she'd asked—not because he was ridiculously good-looking with his chiseled features and his brooding intensity.

He hadn't had to be so curt with her, though. Sure, she'd known he had a limp from an injury in the line of duty. But he still worked as a Cowboy Hero, so she hadn't thought he was really handicapped. He could have held her and just swayed from side to side. It wasn't as if she'd asked him to two-step or line dance with her. But she shouldn't have asked at all. The only reason she had was because of how alone he'd looked…even among all his family.

And that loneliness had called to hers. Because even with her son and her good friends, she sometimes felt alone like that, too. Though that was better than falling for someone only to have them leave.

"I didn't think Forrest was going to stick around much longer," she said. "Won't he move on to the next natural disaster with the rest of the Cowboy Heroes?"

"Whisperwood needs them for more than rescue and recovery efforts right now," Maggie said. She shuddered again. "There's a killer on the loose."

"That's why we should postpone our honeymoon," Bellamy said.

"No," Rae and Maggie said again, their voices soft this time, though.

Bellamy sighed. "Okay, but you both need to promise me that you'll be extra careful."

"Of course," they agreed—again in unison.

"I know Jonah won't let anything happen to you," Bellamy told her sister. "But you…"

Rae smiled. "I can take care of myself." She'd done it most of her life.

Bellamy took the sleeping baby from her arms and snuggled him against her. "But you have Connor to worry about too and your classes. I'm really concerned about you living out there in the country alone."

"I'm not alone," Rae reminded her.

Bellamy pressed another kiss to the soft hair on Connor's head. "He's not going to be much protection against a bad guy—at least not for a few more years."

"Like twenty," Maggie added with a chuckle.

"I don't need a man to protect me," Rae said. She'd never had one. Her father had been more likely to put her and her mother in danger—at least financially— than to protect them. "I don't need a man at all."

"You proved that by having this little guy on your own," Maggie said. "I admire you."

"Me, too," Bellamy added. "Although I think I had more fun conceiving mine the way we did."

Rae stared at her friend. "What?"

"I'm pregnant," the new bride announced, her face glowing with happiness and love.

Tears rushed to Rae's eyes. "That's wonderful."

"So wonderful," Maggie agreed as her eyes filled with tears, too. "I'm thrilled for you."

"Me, too," Rae said. "You and Donovan are going to be amazing parents."

"I'm going to drive you crazy," Bellamy warned her, "with all the questions I'll be asking you." Bellamy's mom was gone, like Rae's was.

Rae missed her every day. They'd been so close. Georgia had been more a friend than a mother to her. Now that she was a mother herself, she'd never needed her more.

"You won't drive me crazy at all," Rae assured

her. "I'm not sure I'll have all the answers, though."
Mostly she felt as if she was stumbling around in the
dark, blindly finding her way as a parent and as a
student again at thirty-five.

"You'll have more than I'll have," Maggie said.
"You're the smartest, most independent person I
know."

The tears already stinging her eyes threatened to
spill over, but Rae blinked them back to smile at her
friend. "I'm not sure about smartest. Law school is
tougher than I thought it would be."

"Because you just had a baby two months ago and
you're working," Bellamy reminded her as she stared
down at Connor, who slept so peacefully in her arms.

If only he slept that peacefully at night...

"It'll get easier," Rae said. That was what she kept
telling herself.

Bellamy chuckled softly. "You're smart, but I think
it's your stubbornness that keeps you going."

A smile tugged at the corners of Rae's mouth. She
couldn't deny that.

"Just don't be so stubborn and independent that you
put yourself in danger," Bellamy advised. "Promise?"

Rae sighed. "Of course I'm not going to put myself
or Connor in danger," she assured her. "Stop worrying about me. And let's get you ready for your honeymoon!"

"Since she's already pregnant, I think she knows
about the birds and the bees," Maggie teased.

They all laughed, which roused Connor from his
impromptu nap. But he didn't cry when he awakened,

just groggily looked up at Bellamy holding him. She was like an aunt to him, and Maggie was fast becoming like another. These women and her baby were all the family that Rae needed.

She didn't need a man for protection or for anything else. But when she left Bellamy's cute two-bedroom house and headed home with Connor safely buckled into the back seat, an odd chill passed through her despite the warmth of the August night. Fear...

Maybe it was all the talk of bodies and killers.

Or maybe it was her postpartum hormones.

She preferred to blame the hormones. Because she had nothing to fear...

The television screen illuminated only the area of the dark room around the TV. From the shadows, he watched the evening news report from the crime scene at Lone Star Pharma.

Her body had been found. His hands clenched into fists as rage coursed through him.

*Damn it...*

The news crews had been kept back—behind the police barricade. But the camera zoomed in on the scene and captured the people investigating the discovery. The Cowboy Heroes...

What the hell were they doing there?

He unclenched one fist to push up the volume button.

"Chief Thompson has enlisted the help of former Austin cold case detective Forrest Colton," the reporter announced. "Colton has been given special dispensation from the Whisperwood Police Department to lead the investigation of this murder and the body discovered last month in a mummified condition. Colton holds the highest clearance rate in the Austin Police Department, so an arrest seems imminent."

He cursed again.

No. An arrest was not imminent. Forrest Colton might have gotten lucky in Austin, but his luck was about to run out in Whisperwood. And maybe his life, as well...

# Chapter 2

A week had passed since his brothers had ambushed him at the crime scene. A week of frustration that gripped Forrest so intensely he wished he'd never accepted the position no matter how temporary it was going to be.

The hurricane had caused so much damage and not just physically. Emotionally people were dealing with the loss of loved ones and their homes or their livelihoods. The Whisperwood police department was stretched thin. The crime scene department was understaffed and the techs were overworked, so nothing had been processed yet from either scene. And the coroner…

She hadn't even taken the bodies from their refrigerated drawers yet let alone begun the autopsies.

And until he had more information, Forrest hadn't wanted to parade in the family members of every missing person to see if the dead woman was their loved one. He didn't want to put every family through that kind of pain.

Hell, he didn't want to put one family through that kind of pain. But it was inevitable. Once they figured out who she was.

Everybody expected miracles from Forrest, but his hands were nearly as tied as the poor victim's hands had been—bound behind her back.

He wrapped the reins around his hands and clenched his knees together as the quarter horse he rode scrambled over the uneven ground. Despite taking the detective position, Forrest continued as a volunteer for the Cowboy Heroes. The team was not done with Whisperwood and the surrounding area, which had been hit particularly hard with flooding after Hurricane Brooke.

The water had begun to recede, though, leaving only muddy areas like the one in which the horse's hooves slipped. His mount leaned, and Forrest nearly slipped off it into the mud. Ignoring the twinge of pain in his bad leg, he tightened his grip.

"Whoa, steady," Forrest murmured soothingly. When the horse regained its balance, a sigh of relief slipped through Forrest's lips. This was why he usually handled the desk work for the rescue agency and not the fieldwork. But like his brothers, he'd been born to the saddle. He couldn't *not* ride.

He wasn't able to help with the rescues as physically as he would have liked, though. Sometimes his leg wouldn't hold his weight let alone the weight of another person or animal. He sighed again but this time with resignation. It was what it was.

He'd accepted that a while ago. And he helped out where he could—like riding around to survey the areas. There were still some people missing, and maybe the floodwaters had hidden their remains.

Not that he wanted to find any more bodies...

But that was the purpose of the recovery part of the Cowboy Heroes rescue and recovery operation. Survivors needed that closure of knowing what had happened to their loved one and having that body to bury. That was why he needed the body in the morgue identified, so he could give her family some small measure of peace.

Until he found her killer...

And he would.

His frustration turning back to determination, he urged the horse across the muddy stretch of land. Heat shimmered off the black shingles of a roof in the distance. He'd started out early from his family ranch, before the sun had even risen much above the horizon, and it wasn't much higher now. So it was going to be another hot August day.

Which was good...

The last of the water should recede and reveal whatever secrets it had been hiding. Whatever bodies—of animals and people.

So much livestock had been lost, too. A pang of regret over all those losses struck his heart. Then another pang of regret struck him when he realized whose house he'd come upon in the country.

*Hers.*

Rae Lemmon. His new sister-in-law's best friend and quite the beauty. He hadn't lived in Whisperwood for years, but he remembered this was her family home. And maybe he'd subconsciously headed that way.

But why? Sure, she was beautiful, but because she was beautiful, she wouldn't want anything to do with a disabled man. She'd asked him to dance at the wedding but that must have only been out of pity or maybe just a sense of obligation to her friend.

And maybe that was why he'd come this way to check on her place—out of a sense of obligation. She was his new sister-in-law's best friend, so that almost made her family, too. And as much as the Coltons took care of everyone else, they took extra care of their own.

He knew that because of how everybody had taken care of him after he'd been shot. Well, everybody but one person. But she hadn't been family yet, and after he'd been shot, she'd returned his ring.

He flinched as the memory rushed over him. Not that he could blame her. As she'd said, she hadn't fallen in love with a handicapped man, so he really shouldn't have expected her to stick around. It wasn't as if they'd said their vows yet, either, and now he expected those vows would not have included in sickness and health.

While the old memories washed over him, the

horse continued on across the muddy field toward the back of the house. The field was higher than the yard, so he could see into it, could see that a tree had toppled over into the water pooled on the grass. Maybe the roots had turned up a mound of dirt, or maybe something else had made the hole. The pile was almost too neat, as if it had been shoveled there.

Maybe she'd thought the hole would drain away the water...

But as Forrest drew nearer, he peered into the hole and discovered it wasn't water filling it. Something else lay inside it, something all swaddled up in linen material smeared with mud and grime.

"What the hell..." he murmured.

He swung his leg over the saddle and dismounted. His boot slipped on the muddy ground, but he used the horse to steady himself. Like all the horses for the Cowboy Heroes, Mick was well-trained and helpful. Forrest patted his mane in appreciation before stepping away from his mount and turning toward the hole. He leaned over and peered inside it, and his boot slipped again.

This time he didn't have the horse to catch himself, so his leg—his bad leg—went out from beneath him. As he began to fall, he reached out to catch himself. But like his boot, his fingers slipped on the mud, too, and he slid into the hole, knocking the loose dirt into it with him. It sprayed across that weird material.

Whatever it was, it had contoured to the shape of the object beneath it. But it wasn't an object...

It was a body with arms and legs and a face...

A mummy, like the one his brother Jonah had found. But unlike that body, Forrest suspected the storm hadn't turned up this one. Someone else had either dug it up or dug the hole to bury it here like someone had buried the woman by the pharmaceutical company.

But why here? Why in Rae Lemmon's backyard?

Forrest reached into his pocket and pulled out his cell phone. He needed to call in a team to process the scene. Hopefully he could remove himself from it without compromising any evidence. After he called out the coroner and some crime scene techs, he shoved his phone back in his pocket and tried to pull himself out of the hole. Using his good leg, he dug his boot into the side of the hole and climbed out. As he pulled his boot free, some dirt tumbled down into the hole next to the body, and the sun glinted off it.

It wasn't just dirt. There was something shiny beneath the mud and grime. Something metallic. Like coins or...

*Buttons?*

Had those belonged to the victim or the killer?

Rae closed her eyes and savored the silence. She would have to get up soon for work, but she had a few minutes to rest her eyes and relax. And after Connor had spent most the night crying inconsolably, she needed some peace. He'd finally fallen back to sleep.

The pediatrician suspected the baby had colic for which Rae blamed herself. The stress of law school, her job and single parenthood had affected her ability to produce breastmilk and she'd had to supplement with formula. When she'd called the doctor's service last night, she'd been told to switch to a soy-based formula, which she would do today on her way to bring Connor to day care.

Exhaustion gripped her, pulling her into oblivion. She had only been asleep for a moment when a noise startled her. It wasn't the light beep of the alarm, but a loud pounding at a door. Worried that the knocking would wake up Connor, she rushed out of her bedroom without bothering to grab a robe. The only people who visited her were Bellamy and Maggie. Maybe Bellamy was back.

But she probably would have just let herself in; she knew where the key was hidden. Disoriented for a moment from lack of sleep, Rae rushed to her front door and opened it. But nobody stood on her porch. If someone was there, they probably would have rung the bell.

The back door rattled as that fist pounded again. And a soft cry drifted from the nursery. Connor wasn't fully awake, but he was waking up. She ran across the living room and kitchen to pull open the door. "Shhh…" she cautioned her visitor. Then she gasped when she recognized the man standing before her. "What—what are you doing here?"

What the hell was he doing there? Especially now?

She had to look like death—after her sleepless night—with dark circles beneath her eyes and her hair standing on end. And her nightgown…

She glanced down at the oversize T-shirt an old

boyfriend had left. At least she'd gotten something comfy out of the relationship. But she hadn't expected much. Her father had taught her to never count on a man sticking around, and every boyfriend she'd ever had had reinforced that lesson.

That was why she'd chosen to be a single mother. She didn't need a husband to have a family. She didn't need a man. But this one...

He was so damn good-looking even with mud on his clothes and smeared across his cheek. A frisson of concern passed through her. "Did you get thrown?" she asked. Over his shoulder—his very broad shoulder—she caught a glimpse of a dark horse pawing at the muddy grass. "Are you okay?"

"I did not get thrown," he said, his voice sharp as if she'd stung his pride.

Or maybe that was just the way he always talked. He'd sounded that way when he'd told her that she couldn't be serious about asking him to dance.

Her face heated with embarrassment, but she didn't know if it was because of what had happened then or how unkempt she looked now. And with the way he kept staring at her, he couldn't have missed her unruly appearance. He was probably horrified.

"Then what are you doing here?" she asked again.

"I've called the police."

"I thought you were the police," she said. She knew, from the news reports and the gossip around Whisperwood, that the chief and his brothers had successfully talked him into investigating the murders.

"I am," he said. "That's why I called. I need to tape off your backyard. It's a crime scene."

Despite the heat of the August day, a cold chill raced down her spine and raised goose bumps on her skin. "Crime scene?" she asked. "What are you talking about?"

"I found something in your yard," he said.

"Why were you searching my property?" she asked. "Did you have a warrant?"

His face flushed now.

"I know my rights," she said. "If you didn't have a warrant, your search was illegal."

"I was surveying the flood damage," he said, "and your yard was in plain view from the field behind it."

Which was his family's property. In Whisperwood, the Coltons' ranch was second in size only to the Corgan spread.

"So you weren't even acting as a lawman when you performed this illegal search?" she asked. "You were just riding around your own property?"

His brow furrowed, and he opened his mouth to answer her, but she cut him off with an, "How dare you!"

She'd thought she'd let it go—her embarrassment over how he'd rejected her request to dance. But now that embarrassment turned to anger, which she unleashed on him.

Or maybe her exhaustion had made her extra irritable.

"You're trespassing on my property," she continued.

"And when your fellow officers arrive, they will be obligated to issue you a citation."

"Rae—"

"You're not above the law," she said, "just because you're a Colton."

"I know I'm not above the law," he said, his face still flushed but with anger now. It burned in his hazel eyes, as well. "And neither are you."

"I am a law student," she said. "And I'm already working as a paralegal. I probably know the law better than you do."

He snorted then. "I've been a police officer for years," he reminded her. "I know the law. Why did *you* switch from managing the general store to law?"

She narrowed her eyes and studied his handsome face. He'd barely talked to her at her friend's and his brother's wedding. Why was he curious about her now? Especially since he seemed to know more than she'd realized about her.

She was proud of her decision to go to law school, so she answered him, "I want to do something about all the crimes happening around Whisperwood."

"Then you should want me to investigate what I found on your property," he pointed out.

Now she was curious, which she probably would have been right way if she wasn't so damn exhausted. "What did you find?" she asked.

"A body."

She gasped in shock and shook her head. "No…" It wasn't possible. Someone couldn't have been murdered in her yard, where she'd imagined her son playing as he grew up like she had played. She shuddered and murmured again, "No…"

Forrest nodded. "I'm afraid it's true."

"But—but I didn't hear anything." Wouldn't she have heard something if someone had been murdered in her backyard? But with work and school she was gone so much that she probably hadn't even been home when it had happened. "I didn't see anything amiss."

"Have you missed anyone?" he asked. "Somebody staying with you that suddenly disappeared?"

She shook her head. Somebody had disappeared years ago on Rae, but that had been his choice to leave. Nobody had murdered him, although she'd sometimes wished she had when she'd watched her mother suffer.

"So you didn't notice anything in the backyard? Any digging?" He persisted with his questions.

She shook her head again. "Why the hell would someone bury a body in my backyard?"

"I'm not sure if they'd just buried it, or if it was just uncovered," Forrest said. "It could have been there awhile."

"Like the body that Maggie and Jonah found after the hurricane?" she asked.

They had just stumbled across the body—the mummified body. She shivered with revulsion. What if that was what Forrest had found in her yard? Another mummy?

"I'll know more once the coroner arrives," he continued.

A siren wailed as it grew closer to her house. Maybe the coroner was arriving now—along with the squad cars with the flashing lights that were pulling into her driveway, as well.

Connor cried out now, and it wasn't a sleepy little cry but a wail almost as loud as the siren.

"What the hell is that?" Forrest asked in alarm.

And Rae bristled all over again with outrage. "*That* is my son," she replied as she hurried off to the nursery.

Tension gripped the chief, and he tightened his grasp on his cell phone before sliding it back into his pocket.

Behind him, sitting on the porch of his two-story farmhouse, Hays Colton chuckled. "Forrest has always had good timing," he said of his son. "You drive out here looking for him, and he calls you like he somehow knew."

Chief Thompson shook his head. "That's not why he called." And he could have pointed out that Forrest's timing wasn't always perfect or young Colton wouldn't have taken that bullet in his leg. But if his instincts weren't as strong as they were, he might have taken that bullet in his heart or his head instead of his leg.

He had survived.

His shooter had not.

"What's wrong?" Hays asked, his blue eyes wide with alarm. "Is he all right?"

Thompson nodded. "Yeah, he just called to give me a heads-up."

"Did he find out the identity of that poor girl found at the pharmaceutical company?"

The chief shook his head. "I wish that was why he called. Or better yet, to tell me he caught the killer." Because it would probably hit the news soon anyway, Archer Thompson shared, "He found another body."

Another person for the already-overworked coroner to identify.

"I'm sorry," Hays said. He rose from the porch swing, set his coffee cup on the railing and reached out to pat Thompson's shoulder.

They'd known each other a long time, but Thompson didn't need any more sympathy. He needed answers—about his sister's murder and about these bodies that had recently turned up. He uttered a ragged sigh as he pushed himself up from the rocking chair in which he'd been sitting. He didn't move as fast as he once had, his bones aching now with age and overuse. He didn't stand quite as straight and tall as he once had.

Neither did Hays, though, who had spent too many of his seventy-some years in the saddle working his ranch. "My son will find out who really killed your sister," Hays assured him.

Thompson wanted to believe the killer was Elliot Corgan—because then he would have the satisfaction of knowing the sick bastard had died in prison. But Elliot had denied killing his sister, and there was no way he could have killed that woman whose body had been discovered in the Lone Star Pharma parking lot.

There was another killer in Whisperwood.

And until he was caught, the chief had a feeling that bodies would keep turning up.

Need an adrenaline rush from nail-biting tales
(and irresistible males)?

Check out **Harlequin Intrigue®**,
**Harlequin® Romantic Suspense** and
**Love Inspired® Suspense** books!

**New books available every month!**

**CONNECT WITH US AT:**

Facebook.com/groups/HarlequinConnection

 Facebook.com/HarlequinBooks

 Twitter.com/HarlequinBooks

 Instagram.com/HarlequinBooks

 Pinterest.com/HarlequinBooks

ReaderService.com

**ROMANCE WHEN
YOU NEED IT**

SGENRE2018R

# *Love Harlequin romance?*

## DISCOVER.

Be the first to find out about promotions, news and exclusive content!

Facebook.com/HarlequinBooks

Twitter.com/HarlequinBooks

Instagram.com/HarlequinBooks

Pinterest.com/HarlequinBooks

ReaderService.com

## EXPLORE.

Sign up for the Harlequin e-newsletter and download a free book from any series at **TryHarlequin.com.**

## CONNECT.

Join our Harlequin community to share your thoughts and connect with other romance readers!
**Facebook.com/groups/HarlequinConnection**

**ROMANCE WHEN
YOU NEED IT**

HSOCIAL2018

SPECIAL EXCERPT FROM

# ⟨H⟩HARLEQUIN®

## ROMANTIC suspense

*Paramedic Remo DeLuca finds Celia Poller on the side
of the road after a car accident. Severely injured,
Celia has short-term memory loss and the only thing
she's sure of is that she has a son—and that someone
is threatening both their lives!*

*Read on for a sneak preview of
Melinda Di Lorenzo's next thrilling romance,*
First Responder on Call.

Remo took a very slow, very careful look up and down
the alley. The side closest to them was clear. But the
other? Not so much. Just outside Remo's mom's place,
the man Celia had so cleverly distracted was engaged in
a visibly heated discussion with another guy, presumably
the one from the car his mother had noted.

Remo drew his head back into the yard and hazarded
a whisper. "Company's still out there. We can wait and
see what happens, or we can slip out and make a run for
it. Move low and quick along the outside of the fence."

Celia met his eyes, and he expected her to pick the
former. Instead, she said, "On the count of three?"

He couldn't keep the surprise from his voice. "Really?"

She answered in a quick, sure voice. "I know it's
risky, but it's not like staying here is totally safe, either. A
neighbor will eventually notice us and give us away. Or
call the police and give Teller a legitimate reason to chase
us. And at least this way, those guys out there don't know

that we know they're here. Right now, they're trying to flush us out quietly."

"As long as you're sure."

"I'm sure."

He put a hand on Xavier's back. "You want to ride with me, buddy?"

The kid turned and stretched out his arms, and Remo took him from his mom and settled him against his hip, then reached for Celia's hand.

"One," he said softly.

"Two," she replied.

"Three," piped up Xavier in his own little whisper.

And they went for it.

*Don't miss*
First Responder on Call *by Melinda Di Lorenzo,*
*available August 2019 wherever*
*Harlequin® Romantic Suspense books*
*and ebooks are sold.*

www.Harlequin.com

# Get 4 FREE REWARDS!

## We'll send you 2 FREE Books plus 2 FREE Mystery Gifts.

**Harlequin® Romantic Suspense** books feature heart-racing sensuality and the promise of a sweeping romance set against the backdrop of suspense.

**FREE** Value Over **$20**